Dead Ringer

THE JACK REACHER EXPERIMENT BOOK 1

Jude Hardin

1

Hundreds of big-rig headlights had whooshed by over the past couple of hours, and there wasn't anything particularly unusual about the pair Wahlman was looking at now.

Except that they were headed straight toward him.

He dove and rolled down the grassy embankment to his left. He half expected the semi to follow him and crush him, but it didn't. It thundered on by, transmitting vibrations all the way down to the bottom of the ditch, tremors that stomped through Wahlman's core like a herd of rhinos. There was no slowing down, no grinding of gears, no screeching of brakes. No indication that a human being was behind the wheel.

Amped on adrenaline, breathing hard, Wahlman clawed his way up the slope, handfuls of slick grass eventually giving way to the gritty pavement at the top.

The massive vehicle continued westward along the shoulder, veering slightly to the right, roguishly, inelegantly, just a stupid machine lumbering through the misty blackness. A machine the size of a house. A machine that would destroy anything in its path.

Wahlman didn't own a cell phone, and there weren't any cars or trucks or motorcycles to flag down at the moment. The interstate had been eerily quiet before the semi approached. No vehicles for several minutes, westbound or eastbound. Wahlman didn't know if it was like that every Sunday at 4:17 in the morning, but he figured it probably was. If you were in Slidell, you probably weren't going to be driving into New Orleans at that hour, and vice versa. You were probably in bed. Maybe one of the lucky ones who could actually sleep through the night every night.

The big truck rolled on. Probably a Freightliner, the way a soft drink is probably a Coke, although it could have been a Kenworth or a Peterbilt or a Mack. Or some other brand. It was pulling a heavy load. You could tell by the hum of the tires on the pavement.

The headlights illuminated a bridge up ahead, a small one built over a canal.

Wahlman figured the truck was traveling at a speed between fifty and sixty miles an hour. Not inordinately fast, but certainly not slow either. Maybe it had been coasting for a while. Maybe the driver had fallen asleep. Or died of a heart attack or something.

Wahlman was standing there wondering exactly what had happened when the semi crashed through the concrete railing that ran along the side of the bridge. The trailer broke loose and toppled cacophonously out into the middle of the highway, showering the pavement with bright orange sparks as the tractor plunged nose-first into the water.

Wahlman wasn't much of a runner. He never had been. He'd played football in high school, but they always put him in a position that didn't require much speed. Offensive line, most of the time. At six feet four inches tall and two hundred forty pounds, there weren't many players who could get past him. In his senior year, a sports reporter at the local newspaper started calling him *Rock*, and the name stuck. He'd been nearly impenetrable on the football field, but he wasn't fast. Not then, not now. He galloped clumsily toward the wreckage, greasy hot steam from the submerged engine rising and meeting him as he finally made it to the edge of the bridge.

The headlight on the driver side was still on, cutting a wedge of brightness into the murky brown canal water. The water wasn't very deep. Eight feet at the most. Wahlman couldn't see into the cab, but he could hear the muffled roar of a classic heavy metal song blaring from the stereo. Nobody could have fallen asleep to that, he thought. Which meant that the driver had lost consciousness some other way. Maybe a cardiac event. Or a stroke. Or something else.

Wahlman pulled his boots off, slid down into the water and peered into the passenger side window. The driver was male, late thirties or early forties, as big as Wahlman, maybe a little bigger. He wore a plaid shirt and a black ball cap. His eyes were closed. There was a thread of blood that started at the corner of his mouth and ended at the edge of his button-down collar. The water inside the cab was up to his chest. Wahlman couldn't tell if he was breathing or not.

Wahlman pounded on the window.

The driver didn't stir.

The music had stopped, and the headlight was getting dimmer by the second.

Wahlman went up for a quick breath of air, and then he dove back down and got on his hands and knees and frantically started searching for something to break the window with. He raked his fingers through the silt, combing a radius of several feet, scooping and grasping at the sandy mud, coming up empty again and again.

He climbed around the engine housing to the other side of the cab, cupped his hands against the window. The water was up to the driver's chin now. Wahlman reared back and hammered the glass with his fist, but it was no use. The resistance from the water prevented the blows from being forceful enough. Maybe he could break through with the heels of his feet, he thought, but he needed to get another breath of air first. He was about to push himself back up to the surface when the driver's eyes opened.

"Help," the guy shouted. "Help me. Please."

Wahlman made a cranking motion with his hand.

"Roll the window down," he said.

Water would flood the cab, violently, like a dam bursting, but then the pressure would equalize and the guy might be able to pull himself out.

"I can't move my arms," the man said.

Every cell in Wahlman's body was screaming for oxygen. He held one finger up to let the driver know he would be right back, and then he surfaced and swam over to the bank. Gasping, coughing, lungs on fire. He grabbed a rock the size of a softball, jumped back into the water and made his way down to the passenger side window. The water was up to the driver's nostrils now. Wahlman started slamming the window with the rock, but the glass didn't break. The water was slowing him down and he was lightheaded and his muscles were starting to fatigue. It felt as though he had been drugged and beaten and thrown into a vat of pancake syrup.

The driver made one last gurgling cry for help as the headlight grew dimmer and dimmer and then went totally black. Wahlman couldn't see anything now. He kept trying to break the window. There was nothing else he could do. He tried several different angles, coming down as hard as he could, gripping the rock with both hands, pounding and pounding and pounding, finally hearing a muffled crack as the safety glass crumpled and folded inward. There was no big gush, as he thought there would be, which meant that the cab was completely full of water now.

Using the rock to grind off any remaining chunks of glass from the window frame, Wahlman managed to climb in and grab the driver by his shirt and pull him out of the truck. The guy was unconscious now. Totally limp. Dead weight. Wahlman struggled to get him into a rescue hold, but it was no use. The man slipped away and sunk to the bottom of the canal like a sack of bowling balls.

Wahlman needed air. He surfaced and took a deep breath, and another, the air warm and wet and heavy, and then he went back down and lifted the driver onto his shoulders, trudged up the slope and heaved the unconscious man onto the rocky bank.

Wahlman was nearly unconscious himself. He coughed out some water and sucked in some air and reached over and pressed two fingers against the side of the man's neck to see if he had a pulse. Nothing. Wahlman struggled to his knees and started chest compressions, noticed right away that the bottom of the man's shirt was soaked with blood.

And then he noticed something else.

The man looked exactly like him.

Same facial features, same hair color, same massive arms and shoulders. The guy had a tattoo on his neck, but otherwise it was like looking into a mirror.

Wahlman continued performing chest compressions.

"Breathe," he shouted.

But the man didn't breathe. And when a thick glob of blackish-red blood oozed out from the center of his mouth, Wahlman decided it was time to stop the resuscitation efforts. He scooted away from the corpse, rolled onto his back, stared up at the diffuse moonlight. A thick blackness engulfed him, and he wondered if he was dying, and he thought he was, and his fingers started tingling and his legs went numb and there was nothing he could do but lie there and let it happen.

2

There was a bright light in Wahlman's face and someone was shaking his shoulder and asking him if he was all right. When he opened his eyes, he saw the silhouette of a police officer standing over him.

He sat up and fought off a wave of nausea.

"I'm okay," he said.

The officer nodded. He slid the flashlight into a compartment on the left side of his belt, between the stun gun and the pepper spray, and then he reached up and keyed the microphone attached to his right epaulet. He announced his unit number and location and told the person on the other end to alert the homicide division and the coroner's office.

"We're going to need a tow truck and a crane and a rescue unit and as many cruisers as you can spare," he said.

The patrolman was young. Twenty-two or twenty-three, Wahlman guessed. Certainly no older than twenty-five. His badge said *NOPD*. New Orleans Police Department. He had pale skin and blue eyes and reddish-blond hair. Five-seven or five-eight, a hundred and fifty pounds at the most. He hadn't been on the job long. Wahlman could tell. He didn't have the air of confidence that came with experience. Maybe this was his first night out in a cruiser by himself. Or maybe this was just the first time he'd worked a major accident.

Wahlman looked up at the bridge. Traffic on the westbound side of the interstate was backed up as far as he could see. A lot of trucks, probably heading into town to make deliveries.

The man who'd been driving the tractor-trailer was still in the same spot on the bank, but he had been covered with a blanket. At least most of him had been covered. The blanket wasn't quite long enough. His mud-caked boots were sticking out of the end closest to the water.

"I tried to help him," Wahlman said to the officer.

"Can you walk, sir?"

"I think so."

"Let's go sit in my car. We can talk there."

Wahlman stood and followed the patrolman up to the shoulder where his cruiser was parked. The officer opened the back door on the passenger side and motioned for Wahlman to get in.

"Why can't I sit up front?" Wahlman asked.

"Against regulations."

"I was an MA in the United States Navy. The only people we put into the backs of cars were suspects. Am I a suspect?"

"I don't know much about the navy," the patrolman said. "But out here in the real world—"

"I was a Master at Arms," Wahlman said. "I was a policeman."

"Then you should know that everyone's a suspect in a situation like this."

"Are you taking me in for questioning?"

"Relax. I just need you to sit here with me until the homicide detective gets here."

Wahlman had an appointment in New Orleans, and he wasn't in the mood to be detained. He knew from experience that these kinds of things could drag on for hours sometimes.

"I'm not getting back there," he said, gesturing toward the back seat of the cruiser. "We can stand out here and talk if you want to."

The officer rested his right hand on the butt of his service pistol. It was a Glock. Probably a .40 caliber. Probably with a 15-round magazine.

"I need you to put your hands on the top of the car and spread your legs apart," the officer said.

"A minute ago we were just going to talk," Wahlman said. "Now you're going to cuff me? Am I under arrest?"

"Hands on top of the car. Now!"

"I haven't done anything wrong. I almost killed myself trying to—"

"Now!"

The officer gripped the pistol and pulled it out of the holster and pointed it at Wahlman's chest. Wahlman glanced down at the barrel, and then he locked eyes with the patrolman.

"What are you charging me with?" he asked.

The policeman's lips trembled.

"Suspicion of murder," he said.

"That's ridiculous. I was just walking along trying to hitch a ride. The truck almost ran me over, and then it crashed through the railing on the bridge. Whatever happened to that driver happened before I ever got to him."

"Either put your hands on the car, or I'm going to add resisting an officer to the charges."

A siren chirped in the distance. Behind the patrolman there was a single blue strobe speeding toward the crash site. Wahlman could see it, but the patrolman couldn't. He was turned the wrong way. He probably didn't hear the siren either. He was too focused on the situation at hand, on what he perceived to be a threat.

"I'm not resisting anything," Wahlman said. "You're nervous and you're not thinking clearly. Pulling your pistol was a mistake. Put it away now and I won't report you for using excessive force."

The patrolman just stood there. He didn't know what to do. Wahlman was obviously unarmed, and he hadn't made any aggressive moves toward the officer. He didn't have any shoes on, so it wasn't like he was going to make a run for it. He hadn't exactly been cooperative, but he hadn't been exceedingly uncooperative either. He just didn't want to get into the back seat of that NOPD cruiser. No door handles, caged off from the front. It was basically a mobile jail cell, and Wahlman hadn't done anything to deserve that sort of treatment, not even for a little while. Not even for one minute.

The car with the single flashing light on the roof steered in behind the cruiser. It was a black sedan. A Chevrolet, Wahlman thought, although he couldn't tell for sure. One sedan looked pretty much like another these days. A man wearing a wrinkled blue suit climbed out. When he saw what was going on, he dropped to one knee and drew his pistol and aimed it at Wahlman's core.

"On the ground," he shouted. "Hands behind your head, fingers laced together. Do it. Now!"

"There's a dead man on the bank," Wahlman said. "I tried to help him, but—"

Wahlman felt a punch in the gut. A split second later, blue arcs of electric pain shot through every muscle in his body. He collapsed to the pavement. He couldn't move. He couldn't talk.

But he could hear.

"Get a pair of cuffs on him," the man in the wrinkled blue suit shouted.

3

While Wahlman had been talking to the man in the wrinkled suit, the patrolman must have gone for his stun gun. The one with the yellow handle. The one next to the flashlight compartment on his utility belt. Wahlman had been zapped with one before, during a training exercise. It wasn't something you wanted to experience twice. Or even once, for that matter.

When Wahlman was able to stand, the patrolman and the man in the wrinkled suit forced him into the back seat of the cruiser. The man in the wrinkled suit climbed in and sat beside him. He was holding a zippered plastic evidence bag that contained the contents of Wahlman's pockets. The patrolman stood outside the door at parade rest.

"You're making a mistake," Wahlman said. "I didn't kill that guy."

"Someone killed him. I took a quick peek under the blanket. His belly's a mess."

"I saw the blood on his shirt. I figured he must have been shot. Or stabbed."

The man in the wrinkled suit nodded.

"Stabbed," he said. "Multiple times."

"Are you charging me with something?"

"Not yet."

"Then take the cuffs off and let me go."

"What's your name?"

Wahlman glanced out the window. Several other police cars had made it to the scene, along with a fire truck and an ambulance.

"I want my stuff," Wahlman said, gesturing toward the evidence bag.

"What's your name?"

"Wahlman. Now let me out of here."

"Got a first name?"

"No."

The man in the wrinkled suit unzipped the bag, reached in and pulled out Wahlman's billfold. It was dripping wet.

"Rock Wahlman," the man in the wrinkled suit said. "Cute. Your parents must have had quite the sense of humor."

"Either charge me with something or let me out of here," Wahlman said, not bothering to tell the man in the wrinkled suit that *Rock* was not the name he'd been given at birth, that he'd legally changed it during his senior year in high school.

The man in the wrinkled suit slid the billfold back into the bag.

"Detective Collins," he said. "New Orleans Police Department, Homicide Division. This is going to go a lot easier on you if you cooperate with us, Mr. Wahlman."

"I already told you. I didn't kill the guy. And I don't know who did kill the guy. End of story. Take the cuffs off and—"

"I noticed the address on your ID. Are you homeless?"

"Why would you assume that?"

"Not many people live in a post office box."

"Maybe it's a really big box."

The detective laughed. "Or maybe you're a really big smartass," he said. "I think we're done here."

Detective Collins tapped on the window. The patrolman opened the door and let him out. They stood there with the door open, probably hoping to scare Wahlman into being a little more cooperative with talk of jail time and so forth. But Wahlman wasn't scared. He was angry. These guys should have been recommending him for a medal or something. Instead they were treating him like a criminal.

"What do you want me to do with him?" the patrolman asked.

"Maybe we can get something out of him over at the station. He failed to provide me with a proper address, which falls under title fourteen, section one-oh-eight. Resisting an officer. He could do up to six months for that. He's obviously some kind of drifter, which makes him a flight risk, so his bail will probably be set pretty high. He won't be going anywhere for a while. I'm going to make some calls, get a couple of divers over here and—"

"You need to go look at the corpse again," Wahlman said.

"Pardon me?" Collins said.

"The guy looks just like me. He could be my twin brother, if I had one. Don't you think there's something just a little bit odd about that?"

"I think there's something just a little bit odd about *you*," Collins said. "We gave you a chance to cooperate, but—"

"You Tased me and cuffed me and threw me into the back of this car for no good reason. Your rookie friend is wearing a body cam, and both your cars have dash cams. I know a good old-fashioned slimeball lawyer who's going to have a field day with this. You'll be lucky to still have a job when I get done with you."

"Don't threaten me, Wahlman."

"It's not a threat, Collins. It's a promise. Go ahead and take me to the station."

"Give me one good reason not to."

"I'll give you two good reasons."

"I'm listening."

"My boots are over there on the bridge. They're still dry. Not possible if I'd been in the cab with the driver. Whoever stabbed him did it east of here, and then got out of the truck. That's the only way it could have happened. Unless he stabbed himself."

Detective Collins glanced pensively over at the wreckage.

"I figured you might have knifed him right before he got to the bridge," he said.

"Why would I have done that?" Wahlman asked. "It would have been tantamount to suicide."

Collins shrugged. "It would have been a stupid thing to do," he said. "But I don't run across too many geniuses in my line of work. I was thinking our divers might be able to find the murder weapon, and of course that still might be the case. But if your boots are on the bridge, and they're dry, then you're right. You're in the clear. You seemed to have worked that out like a pro."

"Believe it or not, I used to be a pretty good cop," Wahlman said. "I might be able to help you get to the bottom of this thing. But I can't do it from a jail cell."

"You were a cop?"

"I was a Master at Arms in the navy. Twenty years of continuous active duty service."

"You're retired? You don't look old enough."

"I enlisted two days after I graduated from high school."

Collins pulled a handkerchief out of his pocket and wiped his nose. His eyes were bloodshot, and he needed a shave.

"I'm going to need your service number," he said. "I can check it out on the computer in my car."

"Not a problem," Wahlman said.

Detective Collins turned back to the patrolman.

"Got a camera?" he asked.

"Sure. On my phone. You're not going to just let him go, are you?"

"Did he tell you he used to be a law enforcement officer?"

"He might have mentioned it. I don't remember."

"Go take some pictures of the victim's face and email them to me," Detective Collins said to the patrolman. "And grab Mr. Wahlman's boots while you're at it."

4

By the time the patrolman made it back with the boots, Detective Collins had already checked on Wahlman's service record.

"Take the cuffs off," Collins said to the patrolman.

"How am I going to write this up?"

"That's your problem."

Wahlman climbed out of the car. The patrolman took the cuffs off.

"Here's how you're going to write it up," Wahlman said, massaging some circulation back into his hands. "You're going to tell the truth. You're going to admit that you overreacted. It's all on camera anyway, so there's point in trying to deny it. You'll probably get some desk time, maybe some remedial training. I'm not going to pursue this any further, but you need to think really hard the next time you decide to pull your gun out and point it at someone."

The patrolman nodded, but he didn't apologize. Not to Wahlman, or to Detective Collins. He didn't say anything. Collins instructed him to file his preliminary report from the computer in his cruiser.

"After that you can get with your sergeant on what to do next," he said.

The patrolman walked around to the driver side of the NOPD cruiser, opened the door, took his hat off and climbed in.

Wahlman sat down on the pavement and started pulling his dry boots on over his wet socks.

"That could have ended badly for all of us," he said.

Collins nodded. "I'm going to go take a look at those pictures," he said. "You're welcome to join me whenever you're ready."

Wahlman finished tying his boots, and then he walked to the passenger side of the unmarked police car, opened the door and slid into the front seat.

"I'm going to need some dry clothes," he said.

"So here's what I don't understand," Detective Collins said. "You're retired from the navy. You get a paycheck every month. So why are you wandering around with no car, no—"

"Who said I don't have a car?"

Collins looked puzzled. "Don't tell me it's at the bottom of the canal," he said.

"It's parked on the shoulder," Wahlman said. "On the other side of Lake Pontchartrain. Black pickup. It died and I couldn't get it started again. The indicator panel is showing a fault at relay fourteen. I hope that's all it is."

"You left it there and started hitchhiking? Why didn't you call for help?"

"I don't have a phone."

"Why not?"

"I don't usually need to call anyone."

Collins laughed. "Got any more surprises for me?"

"I have a house in Florida. And my application for a PI license is pending approval from Tallahassee."

"You want to be a private investigator?" Collins said. "I'm pretty sure you're going to need a cell phone for that job."

"Maybe."

There was a touch-screen computer monitor mounted on the center of the dashboard, the entire device about the size of a hardcover novel. Collins started tapping and swiping, and a few seconds later an image of the dead driver's face appeared on the screen.

Collins stared at the photo for a few seconds, and then he turned and looked at Wahlman. He went back and forth a few times, the expression on his face changing from neutral to something close to astonishment.

"Unbelievable," he said. "The guy looks just like you."

"Except for this," Wahlman said, sliding his fingers along the curved length of faded scar tissue that ran from his right cheek bone to the bottom of his jaw.

"Yeah," Collins said. "Except for that."

"It's possible that he really is my twin brother."

Collins looked puzzled again. "Okay, so when I asked you if you had any more surprises for me—"

"I grew up in an orphanage," Wahlman said. "I don't remember anything about my mother and father. It's possible that I have siblings that I don't know anything about."

Detective Collins reached into one of his pockets and pulled out a pack of chewing gum, one of the expensive retro brands made from real sugar. He offered Wahlman a stick. Wahlman said no thanks.

"Let's say this guy is your twin brother," Collins said, peeling away the foil wrapper and folding a piece of the chewing gum into his mouth. "What are the odds of something like this happening the way it did? You know? What are the odds?"

"Slim to none, I guess," Wahlman said. "Yet it happened."

Collins scrolled through some more pictures of the deceased truck driver.

"What happened to your parents?" he asked.

"They died in a car accident when I was two."

"You were in the car with them?"

"I was. My face got slammed into the radio."

Collins clawed at the stubble on his chin. "So you don't remember anything about having a brother?" he asked.

"How much do you remember from when you were two?"

"Good point."

"Like I said, I don't even remember my parents."

"Their name was Wahlman?"

"As far as I know."

"Ever try to get in touch with anyone? Grandparents? Aunts? Uncles? Cousins?"

"Why should I? They knew where I was. I spent sixteen

years in that shithole. Not one person ever came to see me. Not a single one. I could have used some family back then. Now I don't care."

Collins tapped on the computer screen.

"I just got an email with some information on the driver," he said.

"Let's take a look," Wahlman said.

"Sorry. It's confidential."

"This guy might be my brother."

"I still can't share his personal information with you. Not yet."

"When?"

"We'll need to notify his next-of-kin. Then we can release the information to the media."

"I have to wait to hear about it on the news?"

"Is there somewhere I can reach you?" Collins asked.

"I have hotel reservations. But I don't have any way to get there."

"Where are you staying?"

Wahlman told him the name of the hotel.

"It's on St. Charles Avenue," Wahlman said. "Near the French Quarter."

"I'll make sure you get a ride," Collins said.

Wahlman climbed out of the car, leaned on the fender and waited. A state trooper pulled up about ten minutes later and drove him into New Orleans, exiting the interstate at Canal Street.

5

Wahlman made it to the hotel a little after seven. He checked in, asked for a toothbrush and a razor and some toothpaste and some shaving cream. The guy at the desk didn't say anything about the way he looked or the way he smelled or the condition of the dollar bills he pulled out of his wallet when he asked for change. He took the elevator to the fourth floor, found his room, unlocked the door and walked inside.

It wasn't a fancy place, but it was nice. There was a king size bed against one wall, and a long wooden unit that served as a desk and a dresser and a TV stand against the other. Bathroom, closet, ironing board, all the usual stuff.

Wahlman peeled off his damp and sticky clothes and took a shower. He shaved and brushed his teeth, and then he took another shower, scrubbing himself until it hurt. He wrapped a towel around his waist, carried his dirty things down the hall to the laundry room, fed some quarters into the detergent dispenser and then some more into the washing machine. He returned to his room and watched the news for a while, and then he went back and loaded everything into the dryer.

As he was turning to leave, a woman carrying a white plastic laundry bag walked into the room. Mid-thirties, long black hair, green eyes, olive complexion. She was very attractive. She seemed startled at first, and then embarrassed.

"Oh, excuse me," she said, keeping her eyes on the bag of dirty clothes as she set it on the shelf beside the washing machine.

"I was hoping nobody would be up this early," Wahlman said. "I don't usually go around with nothing but a towel on."

"I was hoping the same thing," the woman said, picking the items of clothing out of the bag one-by-one and dropping them into the washing machine. "That nobody would be up this early, that is."

"Well, take care," Wahlman said.

He went back to his room, watched the news some more. They were talking about the fatal accident on the interstate, but they weren't giving out any details about the driver. Westbound traffic was still backed up for several miles.

Wahlman decided to close his eyes for thirty minutes or so while his clothes dried. He thought about setting the alarm clock on the nightstand, but he didn't. When he woke up, it was almost one o'clock in the afternoon.

In the distance, someone was pounding on a bass drum. *Boom, boom, boom, boom.* Probably a parade somewhere nearby, Wahlman thought. He'd heard that they have a lot of them in New Orleans.

He wrapped the towel around his waist again and walked

back down to the laundry room. His things were on top of the dryer. Someone had folded them for him. Pants, shirt, socks, underwear. There was a note on top of the stack:

I needed the dryer. Your stuff wasn't quite dry, by the way. You owe me fifty cents.

—Allison, room 427

Wahlman picked up his things and walked back to his room and got dressed. He looked out the window. He still couldn't see the parade, but he could tell that it was getting closer. *Boom, boom, boom, boom.* After everything that had happened earlier, his body felt a little bit like that. Like something that had been beaten with mallets.

He emptied his wallet and spread some things out on the dresser to dry. Cash, driver's license, bank cards, proof of insurance. There were a variety of business cards that he'd accumulated over the past couple of years, along with dozens of receipts from restaurants and filling stations. Some of the business cards had phone numbers on the backs of them, none of which were legible anymore. He tossed the ruined items into the trash can, feeling like some kind of pathological packrat for hanging onto them in the first place.

He was about to leave the room when the phone started ringing. He picked up and said hello.

"Detective Collins, NOPD Homicide Division. How are you, Mr. Wahlman?"

"Better. I slept for a while."

"Good. I was wondering if you could stop by the station tomorrow morning."

"What time?"

"Nine if you can make it. I'm at the District Seven Police Station on Dwyer Road. I just need to go over a few things with you, and I'm going to need a written statement regarding your involvement with the accident this morning."

"I'll be there," Wahlman said.

"Great. See you then."

Wahlman hung up the phone. He slid his room key and his debit card and two quarters into the back pocket of his jeans, and then he walked down to room 427. He knocked. Waited. Knocked again. The deadbolt clicked and the door opened. It was the woman he'd seen in the laundry room earlier. She was the one wearing a towel this time. Her shoulders were the same shade as her complexion. No tan lines, so it wasn't from the sun. It was just her natural color. She smelled wonderful.

"Sorry," Wahlman said. "I just wanted to pay you back for the dryer."

He reached into his pocket and pulled out the quarters and handed them to her.

"Thanks," she said.

"Thanks for folding my clothes."

"No problem. Is this your first time in New Orleans?"

"It is. Why do you ask?"

"No reason. Just curious. Anyway, maybe I'll see you around."

"Okay."

Allison closed the door. Wahlman stood there for a few seconds, and then he took the elevator down to the first floor and used the ATM to withdraw some money from his checking account. Opposite the check-in desk there was an area with dining tables and booths and a counter where you could order food and drinks, and behind all that there was an alcove with some computers set up for guests of the hotel. Wahlman sat down at one of the computers and searched for automotive repair shops. He wrote down some numbers, went back up to his room and made some calls. The first three places didn't answer their phones. The fourth one did, but it was Sunday and they were closing early, and they asked if he could please call back tomorrow. Wahlman finally found a place that was open until seven, but the guy he talked to said that he would need some kind of guarantee of payment before he could send a tow truck way over to Slidell. Wahlman didn't want to give the guy his credit card number over the phone, so he told him to forget about it.

Wahlman went back down to the first floor and asked the guy at the desk if he knew anyone who worked on cars.

"My brother-in-law might be able to help you," the clerk said. "He has a landscaping business, but he does that kind of thing on the side sometimes."

"I'm pretty sure it just needs a relay," Wahlman said.

The clerk pulled a cell phone out of his pocket and punched in a number. Apparently his brother-in-law's name was Sam, and apparently Sam didn't have a lot going on today. He agreed to pick Wahlman up at the hotel, take him to an auto parts store to buy a new relay, and then take him to his truck. All for a hundred dollars. If it wasn't the relay, he would tie a rope to Wahlman's bumper and tow the vehicle to his place over on the West Bank and try to figure out what the problem was at thirty dollars an hour.

Wahlman agreed to those terms.

As it turned out, Relay 14 was indeed the problem, and two hours later Wahlman was back at the hotel with his truck. He pulled to the curb and climbed out and walked inside and arranged for valet parking, and then he trotted over to the sandwich shop across the street, where he was late for an appointment with a man named Drake.

6

It was almost four-thirty in the afternoon, and there weren't many people in the sandwich shop. Too late for lunch, too early for dinner. There was a middle-aged couple at one table and two women who might have been college students at another. Wahlman didn't see any men sitting alone. He walked to the service counter, where he was greeted by a hairy fellow wearing a red t-shirt and a white apron.

"Can I help you?" the man asked. He had a full beard and forearms that looked like Chia Pets.

"I was supposed to meet someone here," Wahlman said. "Was there a guy here earlier who looked like he was waiting for someone?"

"There were lots of guys here earlier."

"I was supposed to meet him about twenty minutes ago. He said he was going to be wearing a Tulane football jersey."

The man shrugged. "I don't know," he said. "You want something to eat?"

Wahlman looked up at the menu mounted on the wall behind the counter. It was possible that Drake was running late too, possible that he might show up in a few minutes.

"How fresh are your oysters?" Wahlman asked.

"Pulled out of the Gulf yesterday. Best in New Orleans."

"Let me have an oyster po'boy and a side of fries."

"Anything to drink?"

"I'll try the Abita," Wahlman said.

The man behind the counter reached into a glass-fronted refrigerator, grabbed a bottle of Abita Amber lager and opened it and rang up the order. Wahlman paid him and carried the beer to a table by the window. The middle-aged couple and the college students must have exited the restaurant while Wahlman was placing his order. Now he had the entire dining area to himself.

It was a nice autumn day, and there were quite a few people out on the street. You could spot the tourists by the way they walked along casually and looked around and pointed at things. Some of them were wearing lanyards with nametags attached to them. Probably attending a conference at one of the big hotels, Wahlman thought. Some of them were carrying plastic cups filled with frozen drinks, and some of them were carrying shopping bags filled with who-knows-what. Some of them were eating hot dogs from street vendors. Everyone seemed to be having a swell time and Wahlman was enjoying his beer and the aroma of the oysters frying and he was wondering what had happened to Drake when four shots rang out and four fat holes suddenly appeared in the big plate glass window.

Wahlman hit the deck and started crawling toward the

service counter. People outside were screaming. Panicking. Undoubtedly scurrying in every direction, trying to make it to safety as more bullets whizzed through the sandwich shop and more glass rained down on the floor.

Wahlman made it to the area behind the counter. The hairy man was back there on the floor nervously fiddling with a cell phone.

"Do you have a gun back here?" Wahlman asked.

"Why would I have a gun?"

"Why wouldn't you?"

"This is a good area," the man said. "We don't have no trouble around here."

And yet there was trouble, Wahlman thought. Big trouble. Those first four shots had come within inches of his face. He'd heard the bullets whistle by. It seemed highly unlikely that this was a random attack. It seemed that whoever was doing the shooting had chosen a target, and it seemed that the target was Rock Wahlman.

The hairy man was on the phone with the 911 dispatcher, explaining what had happened. When he finished, he told Wahlman that there were plenty of knives in the kitchen, and that maybe it would be a good idea to arm themselves in case the bad guys decided to come inside.

"Knives won't do us any good," Wahlman said. "Is there a back door?"

"Yes. On the other side of the kitchen."

"Let's get out of here."

"I need to wait for the police."

The shooting had stopped. Wahlman figured the assassin

was long gone by now. You don't shoot up a restaurant and then hang around outside and wait for the police to arrive. And if you're going to come inside to finish the job, you do it quickly. So the bad guy had probably driven off in a hurry. Then again, some very peculiar things had happened over the past twelve hours, so it probably wasn't wise to rule anything out. It was possible that the shooter was out there reloading, that he or she would stroll in any second and blow Wahlman's and the hairy man's brains out.

"We need to leave," Wahlman said.

"Why? It seems that it would be safer to stay inside."

"Maybe. Maybe not."

"But the police are coming. They'll want to talk to me. And they'll want to talk to you too."

"We can talk to them later. Let's go."

"I'm staying."

"I would advise against it."

"I'm staying."

"Okay."

Wahlman crawled toward the beer cooler and then through the swinging door that led to the kitchen. He found the service door, peeked out first and then walked outside to the alley. It took him a few seconds to get his bearings. He noticed another service door on the other side of the alley. Some kind of pizza place. There was a plastic trash can beside the door and a security camera over it and a fat padlock dangling from its metal frame. Canal Street was to Wahlman's right, and Common Street was to his left. A crowd had gathered along Canal Street for another parade.

The band was marching by, along with dozens of other people, some of them waving bandanas and others dancing along with colorful little paper umbrellas. There was the steady thump of the bass drum, like the one Wahlman had heard earlier, along with trumpets and trombones and a tuba and a snare drum. The spectators and the people marching in the parade obviously hadn't heard the gunshots. They were smiling and swaying to the beat and having a good time. Wahlman started toward Common Street, thinking he would try to walk around the block and enter the hotel from the side, but he hadn't gotten very far when he heard an echoing series of blasts from inside the sandwich shop.

Boom, boom, boom, boom.

Four shots, two from one pistol and two from another. One of the guns was probably a .45 or a nine millimeter, the other something smaller. Wahlman could tell by the sound of the reports. Two different weapons, which meant that there were probably two different shooters.

Wahlman turned around and took off running for Canal Street. Best to try to disappear into the crowd at this point, he thought. He was a head taller than most of the other people, so he bent his knees and his neck and tried to keep a low profile as he made his way over to St. Charles Avenue. He took a right at the intersection and jaywalked across the streetcar tracks and pushed his way through the heavy glass doors at the front entrance of the hotel. The doorman said *good afternoon sir* or something like that and Wahlman nodded and made a beeline for the elevators. When he got to the fourth floor, he started thinking about everything that had happened and how close he'd come to dying—twice—and how you might be able to accept that one of those instances was an outlandish coincidence but not both of them. He started thinking that it might not be such a good idea to go to his own room.

So he didn't.

Instead, he trotted down the hallway past the ice machine and the vending machines and the laundry facilities and knocked on the door to room 427.

7

Allison answered the door.

"I'll give you a hundred dollars if you let me borrow your room for a while," Wahlman said.

"Excuse me?"

"Some very bad people are after me. I need a place to hide."

"I'm sorry, but—"

Wahlman moved forward, sidestepped his way past the threshold and closed the door behind him.

"You don't understand," he said. "They're trying to kill me."

"Are you out of your mind? You can't just barge into my room like this."

"I'll make it up to you. I promise. I just need your help for a little while."

Allison's purse was on the bed. She walked over there and unsnapped the front flap and pulled out a cell phone.

"I'm calling the police," she said.

"Good idea. Ask for Detective Collins."

"What are you talking about?"

Wahlman gave her a condensed version of the events that had transpired over the course of the day, starting with the out-of-control diesel rig early that morning and ending with the shooting at the sandwich shop just a few minutes ago.

"So you can see why I didn't want to go to my own room," he said.

"Unbelievable," Allison said.

"I know," Wahlman said.

"No, I mean it's unbelievable that you would slink into my room like you own the place and then try to bullshit me with such a—"

"Call Detective Collins," Wahlman said, stepping toward the window and parting the drapes enough to peek outside. "He's at the Seventh District Police Station. Or maybe he's home by now, but they'll know how to reach him. Collins will verify that everything I've told you is absolutely true."

"What are you looking at?" Allison asked.

"The sandwich shop. It's a crime scene now. Hear the sirens? That's the police and the other emergency vehicles coming. There was only one person working over there when I walked in, one guy ringing up the orders and doing the cooking, one guy taking care of everything while it was slow, between the lunch shift and the dinner shift. I'm guessing he was the owner. And I'm guessing he's dead now."

"If that's true, how do I know you're not the one who killed him?"

Wahlman stood there and stared down at the ruined plate glass window.

"You don't," he said.

And neither would the police, he thought. At least four witnesses—the middle-aged couple and the two college women—had seen him walk through the front door of the sandwich shop, and nobody had seen him walk out of the front door, because he hadn't walked out of the front door. He'd walked out of the back door. He'd walked out and stared straight into the security camera across the alley, and then he'd started running toward Canal Street. Running away like some kind of criminal, like someone who might have just shot the owner of a sandwich shop. He would be a suspect, for sure. And there were no dry boots to get him off the hook this time.

"I think you better leave my room now," Allison said. "My husband should be back any minute, and—"

"You don't have a husband," Wahlman said. "Or maybe you do, but if so he's not staying here at the hotel with you."

"What makes you so sure about that?"

"I saw you loading your laundry into the washing machine. It was all women's stuff. And there's only one suitcase and one carryon bag over there in the corner. You're here by yourself. Like me."

"You're pretty perceptive," Allison said. "But I really do need you to leave now. I'm going to give you five more seconds, and then I'm calling nine-one-one."

"You don't have a husband here with you, and you're not going to call the police," Wahlman said. "If you were going to call the police, you would have done it by now. My guess is that you have something to hide. I wouldn't want to speculate about what it is, but I'm pretty sure you don't want to talk to the police right now—any more than I do."

Allison sat down on the bed.

"What do you want?" she asked.

"I just want to stay here for a while. I'm pretty sure whoever shot up the sandwich shop was aiming for me. It probably won't take them long to find out my room number. I need to not be there when they come for me."

"Why is someone trying to kill you?"

"That's what I need to find out."

Wahlman was still standing by the window. Two NOPD cruisers were parked in front of the sandwich shop now, blue lights flashing. Allison got up and walked over to the window and peeked out.

"Maybe we should start from the beginning," she said. "Why did you come to New Orleans in the first place?"

"A man named Clifford Terrence Drake contacted me several weeks ago. He wanted me to meet him down there in the sandwich shop at four o'clock this afternoon."

"Why?"

"He's a lawyer. He knew I grew up in an orphanage. Apparently my maternal grandfather passed away recently, and apparently he left me a great deal of money. Drake was in charge of dispersing the funds from the estate."

"You grew up in an orphanage?"

"Yes. My parents died in a car accident."

"I'm sorry."

"It was a long time ago."

"Why the sandwich shop?" Allison asked. "Why didn't Mr. Drake want you to meet him in his office?"

"He said it was being renovated."

"Are you sure he's really a lawyer?"

"I looked him up. He's legit."

"How much money are we talking about?" Allison asked.

"A hundred thousand, according to Drake."

Allison took a deep breath, let it out slowly.

"That's a lot of money," she said.

"It's not exactly life-changing, but it's better than the big fat zero I was expecting."

"But Drake didn't show up for the meeting?"

"He might have. I was running late. He might have given up on me."

Allison walked back over to the bed and sat down. She crossed her legs, laced her hands together, stared down at the gray carpet.

"Maybe Drake was the one who tried to kill you," she said.

"Maybe, but I don't think so. Drake's going to get his percentage no matter how many beneficiaries there are. He wouldn't have had a motive to kill me."

"So it must have been one of your family members," Allison said. "Someone who stood to inherit more money if you were out of the picture."

"That would be the logical conclusion," Wahlman said. "If it was just the incident at the sandwich shop. But it wasn't. Like I told you, a semi almost ran over me this morning. A truck with a driver who looked just like me, a driver who had been stabbed multiple times."

"That's the part that makes absolutely no sense."

"None whatsoever."

"Do you have a phone number for Mr. Drake?"

"I had his cell phone number. It was written on the back of a business card in my wallet. The ink bled when it got wet."

Allison picked up her phone and started tapping and swiping.

"Clifford T. Drake and Associates," she said. "You can use my room phone to make the call."

She told Wahlman the number to Drake's office.

"It's being renovated," Wahlman said. "I doubt if anyone who works in the law office is there. And it's Sunday. So the people doing the renovating probably aren't there either."

"I think most lawyers use an answering service for afterhours and weekends. You could call and leave a message."

"I guess I could. Drake might check his messages from home, or from wherever he is."

"I would think so," Allison said.

Wahlman walked over to the nightstand, picked up the phone and punched in the number, and a recorded voice immediately announced that it was no longer in service.

Drake had told Wahlman that his office was under renovation, but it didn't make sense that his phone had been disconnected. Forwarded to a third-party answering service, perhaps, as Allison had suggested, but not completely disconnected. Most lawyers keep the same office number from the day they hang out a shingle until the day they die. Wahlman had read that in a book one time.

"Let me make sure I dialed the right number," he said.

Allison told him the number again. He punched it in again. Got the recording again.

"Wait a minute," Allison said, staring down at her cell phone. "I think I just found out why Drake's phone was disconnected."

"Why?"

"Because he's dead. I just found his obituary."

"Maybe I talked to his son. Clifford T. Drake Junior."

"He was survived by two daughters," Allison said. "No mention of a son."

She handed her cell phone to Wahlman. He read the first paragraph of the article, and then he noticed the date on it.

"This can't be right," he said. "I talked to Drake two days ago. It says here that he died almost two years ago."

"Maybe he faked his own death," Allison said, her voice taking on a sudden tone of sarcasm. "Sure, that's it. He faked his own death and then he called you out of the blue with promises of great riches. Can't you see that this whole thing was some kind of scam? Clifford T. Drake didn't call you. It was someone *pretending* to be him, someone hoping to scam you out of some money."

"Maybe," Wahlman said. "But the person who contacted me two days ago knew things about me that an ordinary run-of-the-mill con artist just couldn't have known. He knew that I grew up in an orphanage. He knew what kind of car my parents and I were in when we had the accident. He knew what my first name was before I changed it."

"All that means is that he did his research," Allison said. "Some of those operations are incredibly sophisticated these days."

Wahlman walked back over to the window, peeked through the drapes again. Several more police cars had arrived, along with an ambulance and a fire truck. A couple of the NOPD patrolmen were stretching some yellow crime scene tape around the area in front of the restaurant.

"It wasn't a scam," Wahlman said. "Not the kind where someone expects to make some money, anyway. It was a setup. The person pretending to be Drake just wanted to get me inside that sandwich shop at that time of day. It was a hit, pure and simple."

"Shouldn't you be telling the police all this stuff?"

"No. Not until I can prove that I wasn't the one who did the shooting. And the only way to do that is to find the person who *did* do the shooting."

"But if you explain—"

"If I go to the police right now, they'll arrest me. They won't have any choice. Maybe eventually I'll be exonerated. Maybe not. You never know with a case like this."

"So how do you plan on finding the killer?"

Wahlman thought about that for a few seconds.

"Do you have a car?" he asked.

"Yes, but—"

"I'm going to need your help."

Allison shook her head. "No way," she said. "I have my

own problems. I can't just drop what I'm doing and—"

"What kind of problems?" Wahlman asked.

"You don't want to know."

"Maybe we can help each other."

Allison stared down at the floor again. "I don't think so," she said. "Not unless you really are going to inherit that money."

"How much do you need?" Wahlman asked.

"Ten thousand. But it might as well be ten million. I have no way of—"

"Consider it done," Wahlman said. "You help me out for a few days, and I'll give you the money. No questions asked."

"You have ten thousand dollars lying around somewhere?"

"Give or take."

"I need it by Wednesday," Allison said.

"Why Wednesday?"

"I thought you said no questions."

"Fair enough," Wahlman said. "My pension check will be directly deposited into my checking account Tuesday. Once that happens, I'll have a little over ten thousand in the account. I'll pay you Tuesday afternoon."

"How do I know—"

"You don't," Wahlman said. "You're just going to have to trust me."

Allison sat there and stared at the floor some more. Then she looked up at Wahlman and brushed a tear off her cheek and said okay.

8

Wahlman figured it would take the police at least a couple of days to go through all of the video footage from the security cameras in the area, which meant that it would be at least a couple of days before his face was displayed on every news broadcast in the country.

"I'm not too worried about the police seeing me," he said. "They don't know who they're looking for yet. It's the killers I'm worried about. They know what I look like."

"They don't know what I look like," Allison said. "Just let me know what you want me to do."

Wahlman pulled some cash out of his billfold.

"I don't know about you, but I'm starving," he said. "Go out and get us something to eat. And bring back some hair dye and some sunglasses. I need a new shirt and a new pair of pants, and I might want to borrow some of your makeup when you get back."

"Makeup?"

"To cover this scar."

Allison nodded. "I'm going to need some money for gas,

too," she said. "My tank's almost empty, and I maxed out my credit card to get this room for a few days."

Wahlman handed her the rest of his money.

"That should be enough for everything," he said. "I'll hit the ATM again later."

Allison picked up her phone and her purse and walked to the door.

"See you in a little while," she said.

"Okay."

Wahlman secured the deadbolt and the swing bar, and then he walked over to the coffee setup and grabbed the pot and took it to the bathroom and filled it with water. He tore open one of the little packages of coffee and loaded the handy-dandy prefabricated pouch into the filter basket and poured the water into the reservoir. He switched the machine on, and then he walked over to the corner of the room and started inspecting Allison's luggage. It wasn't something that he normally would have done, but he needed to make sure she wasn't hiding something that would put them both in more danger than they were already in.

The big suitcase was empty, and all Wahlman found in the carryon bag was a partial roll of quarters and a bottle of prescription pain tablets and two paperback novels. He fanned through the books to make sure there wasn't anything hidden in the pages, and then he placed everything back the way it was and moved over to the dresser and started opening drawers. He looked through all of them, found nothing out of the ordinary, checked the closet next and found a folded piece of paper in one of the pockets of a brown leather jacket. He carefully unfolded the paper and saw that it was a contract for a loan in the amount of five thousand dollars. If you paid the money back within two weeks, the loan only cost you a grand. Two more weeks and the price went up to twenty-five hundred. And so forth. Allison had been telling the truth about how much she needed. Ten thousand by Wednesday, or the loan went to collections. Maybe a black eye to start with. Maybe a broken bone or two after that. And so forth. Wahlman folded the paper and slid it back into the pocket. He figured it wouldn't be a problem as long as Allison handed over the money in time.

Wahlman walked back over to the coffeemaker and grabbed one of the insulated paper cups from the caddy and unwrapped it and filled it with coffee. He tried to take a sip, but it was too hot. He found the remote and switched on the television, saw that *60 Minutes* was on and realized that it was after seven o'clock and that there probably wouldn't be any local news broadcasts until ten. He tried the coffee again and it was okay and he turned the television off and walked over to the window. Emergency vehicles everywhere. Yellow tape everywhere. There were two police cars parked at the intersection, lights flashing, blocking the traffic turning off Canal Street or coming straight over from Royal Street.

Wahlman finished his coffee, poured himself another cup.

And then the phone started ringing.

Wahlman stood there and stared at it for a few seconds.

Maybe it was Allison. Then again, maybe it wasn't. They should have decided on some kind of code. Ring once, hang up, ring again. Something like that.

Wahlman decided not to answer. He didn't want to talk to anyone. Say it was the front desk, and say a couple of police detectives were down there canvassing for potential witnesses. Allison's room was directly across the street from the sandwich shop, so it was one of the first ones they would call. As long as nobody answered, they would have to assume that Allison was out of the room, and they would have to move on. They would probably try again later, but Allison would be back later and she could tell them she didn't see anything, which happened to be the truth. That was Wahlman's theory—based on his own experience as a law enforcement officer—that the phone would ring eight to ten times and then stop.

But it didn't stop.

It kept ringing.

And ringing.

And ringing.

Then Wahlman remembered. The hair dye. He hadn't told Allison what color to get. Not that it really mattered, but he should have told her something. There was no way for her to know that he didn't care. She was probably calling to ask about that.

Almost certain that a detective working a fresh murder case wouldn't have waited twenty-some rings for someone to answer, Wahlman walked over to the nightstand and picked up the phone and said hello.

"May I speak to Allison Bentley, please?" a male voice said.

Wahlman didn't know which would seem more suspicious—hanging up or talking.

He decided to talk.

"She's not here right now," he said. "Can I take a message?"

"Tell her Mr. Tanner called. Just a friendly reminder."

Dial tone.

Tanner was the name on the loan contract. He was the guy Allison owed money to.

The phone rang again. It was Allison this time, asking about the hair dye. Wahlman told her dark brown, and she was back in the room fifteen minutes later with the dye and a six-pack of beer and the sunglasses and the clothes and a big bag of fried chicken.

Allison opened two of the beers, loaded the others into the little dormitory-style refrigerator by the window. She put a clean bath towel on the center of the bed and spread the food out and they sat there and ate picnic-style. Chicken, slaw, mashed potatoes, biscuits.

"This is good," Wahlman said.

"Have you given any thought to how you're going to go about finding the people who shot up the sandwich shop?"

"They didn't just shoot up the sandwich shop. They killed the owner."

"You know that for sure?"

"I heard four gunshots soon after I exited the building."

"Maybe they were just trying to scare the guy."

"Are you always so optimistic?" Wahlman asked.

"Are you always so pessimistic?"

"Not always. Anyway, we'll know for sure at ten o'clock when the news comes on."

"You never did answer my question. Have you given any thought—"

"Someone called here a while ago," Wahlman said. "A man named Tanner. He said something about it being a friendly reminder. Then he hung up."

"I'll call him back later. You still didn't answer my question."

"I need to sleep on it."

"Which brings up another subject," Allison said. "I hope you don't think—"

"Don't worry," Wahlman said. "I'll sleep on the floor."

"I guess I could ask for a rollaway bed."

"I would prefer to keep our little arrangement a secret. Eventually the police will be over here conducting interviews, so it's best that the management doesn't know you have a guest."

"Okay. Whatever you want."

They finished the chicken and opened two more beers and looked out the window for a while. Wahlman decided to go ahead and dye his hair and try some of Allison's makeup on his face. He took his shirt off and walked over to the vanity in the little alcove that led to the bathroom and emerged an hour later looking like some kind of department store mannequin. Extra- large, extra-creepy.

"What do you think?" he asked, laughing. "Tell the truth

now."

"I think maybe I better help you," Allison said.

She went to the vanity with him and washed the makeup off and scrubbed some of the dye out of his hair. She toweled him off and put him in the desk chair and sat on the edge of the bed and reapplied the makeup.

"I feel like I'm getting ready to go on TV or something," Wahlman said.

"This is the first time I've ever put makeup on someone else. I'm sure I'll get better with practice. Anyway, this is better than it was. Want to take a look?"

Wahlman got up and walked to the vanity and looked in the mirror. The transformation was remarkable. He barely recognized himself.

"I think you did a great job," he said.

"Thanks. It's almost ten o'clock. Did you want to watch the news?"

"Yes."

Allison turned the television on, and a few minutes later they learned that the man who'd been working alone in the sandwich shop was indeed the owner.

And they learned that he was in the hospital in critical condition.

9

Wahlman woke up at 5:27 a.m.

He always woke up at 5:27, regardless of the time he went to bed. It was the time he'd always set his alarm clock for when he was in the navy. The last several years, anyway, after he'd been promoted to Senior Chief and didn't have to work any of the night watches anymore.

He put his new clothes on, khaki pants and a striped polo, made sure the makeup Allison had applied last night was still covering the scar, left the room and took the stairs down to the first floor. He exited the hotel through the side door, hoping to avoid any contact with the staff.

One of the housekeeping associates was out on the sidewalk smoking a cigarette, but she was busy thumbing a text message into her cell phone and didn't seem to pay any attention to Wahlman as he sauntered by and made his way out to the street.

It seemed to Wahlman that for the past few decades a good percentage of the world's population had been injected with a toxic dose of distraction. *Amazing technology*, they called it. Cell phones, tablet computers, navigation systems. Eyeglasses with holographic video displays. Wrist watches that monitored everything from your heart rate to your sleep cycles—and even your thoughts, according to some of the wilder conspiracy theories. Wahlman doubted that the technology was quite that advanced yet, although it was probably only a matter of time. At least the ubiquitous electronic devices made it relatively easy to walk around and not be noticed, he thought.

Allison had set her alarm clock for seven, and Wahlman figured it would be at least eight before she was ready to do anything. He found a coffee shop on Canal Street, used the ATM by the door to withdraw some money, ordered a large cup to go and asked the barista how to get to the hospital.

"You mean University?" she asked.

"Yes."

"It's about a mile up that way. Just past the interstate on the left."

"Will the streetcar take me there?"

"Sure."

Wahlman paid her, walked up to the next corner and waited for the streetcar. The first one that came by was full, but the one behind it had plenty of space. Wahlman climbed aboard and paid the driver and found a vacant seat near the back. Solid wood benches, naked light bulbs, cords you pulled when your stop was coming up.

Windows that you could lower if you needed some fresh air.

Point A to Point B with no air pollution and very little

noise.

Engineering that had been around for almost two hundred years.

Wahlman wondered why more cities didn't use streetcars. He guessed they weren't amazing enough.

He got off and crossed the street and made his way through the revolving glass door at the front entrance of the hospital and stopped at the information desk. A woman wearing a navy blue dress and an expensive set of fingernails asked how she could help him this morning.

"I wanted to check on a patient named Walter Babineaux," he said.

"Are you family?"

"Just a friend."

The woman clicked her mouse and tapped her keyboard, the fake nails adding a whispery plastic-on-plastic sound that Wahlman found incredibly attractive for some reason.

"He's in the Intensive Care Unit on the eighth floor," she said. "All I can tell you right now is that he's stable."

"Would it be possible for me to go up and visit him?"

"Sorry. Family only. Anyway—and I really shouldn't be telling you this—he hasn't regained consciousness yet. So I'm afraid it wouldn't be much of a visit, even if you were allowed."

"Okay. Thanks."

Wahlman walked over to a gigantic window that overlooked Canal Street, sat on a padded bench and sipped his coffee, which had finally cooled off enough to drink. He had wanted to ask Babineaux if he had seen the people who shot him. A physical description would be useful in identifying them if they happened to show up in the area around the hotel again.

And Wahlman was almost certain they would.

The local news channels were calling the attack on the sandwich shop an armed robbery. Addicts desperate for a fix, maybe. But Wahlman knew better. They might have taken some money on the way out to make it look like some kind of heist, but their primary purpose had been to eliminate Rock Wahlman.

And leave no witnesses.

Which meant that Walter Babineaux was still in great danger.

Wahlman wondered if the police department had posted a guard outside his room. If not, they needed to. Family only, the woman at the desk had said, but hired assassins probably weren't overly concerned with hospital rules. They would find a way to get to Babineaux, to make sure he never woke up.

Wahlman walked around the first floor of the hospital until he found a payphone. He asked the operator for the non-emergency number for the New Orleans Police Department, dropped some money into the slot and made the call. The officer who answered identified himself as Sergeant Dobbs.

"There's a man named Walter Babineaux in ICU at University," Wahlman said. "I have reason to believe that the people who put him there still pose a threat. He needs a guard outside his room around the clock."

"Your name, sir?"

"This is an anonymous call. I just wanted to make sure you know what you're dealing with."

"We appreciate your concern, sir. Thanks so much for calling."

Sergeant Dobbs hung up.

Wahlman called the number again. Dobbs answered again.

"You shouldn't blow me off," Wahlman said. "I know what I'm talking about."

"Sir—"

"I know. It's an ongoing investigation, and you can't discuss any of the details over the phone. But here's the thing: the media's calling it an armed robbery. It wasn't. It was an assassination attempt. I know this because I was the intended target. I was sitting there looking out the window when four bullets whizzed by my head. Walter Babineaux had nothing to do with anything. I just happened to walk into his sandwich shop instead of someone else's. But he's a witness now, and the people who shot him aren't going to be happy that he's still alive. He needs protection."

"If what you're saying is true, it sounds as though you might need protection as well," Dobbs said. "Come to the station and identify yourself, and—"

"I can't do that," Wahlman said. "Not right now. But if you give Babineaux the protection he needs, he can verify my story when he wakes up."

Dobbs started saying something about how much the department depended on ordinary citizens to come forward in cases like this, started rambling on and on about it, kept talking while Wahlman wiped his fingerprints off the receiver and left it dangling and walked back out to the streetcar stop. As he was boarding for the ride back to the hotel, he saw two NOPD cruisers pull to the curb in front of the hospital.

Probably sent by the suddenly-talkative Sergeant Dobbs to apprehend him, he thought.

10

Allison was already downstairs when Wahlman got back to the hotel, sitting at a booth in the little bistro opposite the front desk. There was a crumpled copy of the *Times-Picayune* on the seat beside her. Wahlman could see that she had been working on the crossword puzzle.

"So what's on the agenda for today?" she asked, stirring some creamer and artificial sweetener into her coffee.

"I'm supposed to meet with Detective Collins at the District Seven Police Station," Wahlman said.

"I thought you were avoiding the police."

"I'm avoiding them in regard to the shooting yesterday. There's no way for Collins to know I was involved in that, not until the detectives working the shooting go through all the video, which should take at least a couple of days. Collins is in charge of the case involving the murdered truck driver."

"The one who looked just like you."

"Yes. The one who was stabbed to death, undoubtedly by the same people who tried to shoot me at the sandwich shop. If I can learn the driver's identity, it might help in establishing a motive, which eventually might help in tracking down the killers."

"Have you thought about trying to get in touch with someone from your biological family? You know, to see if you had a twin brother?"

"That's next on the list. First I need to talk to Collins. My appointment's at nine o'clock, so we need to get going."

They left the hotel, made it over to Dwyer Road a little before nine. The police station looked like something a kid had put together with blocks. Some of the big concrete cubes had been painted a color that might have looked good on a 1956 Ford or the walls of a nursery when you knew it was going to be a boy. Allison parked the car in the visitors' lot and waited there while Wahlman climbed out and headed toward the front entrance. He was a little nervous about the meeting, because it was possible that the security videos from the area around the sandwich shop had been circulated already, possible that the desk sergeant would activate some kind of alarm as soon as he walked in the door.

But that didn't happen.

"Can I help you?" the sergeant asked.

"I have an appointment with Detective Collins," Wahlman said. "I'm a little early."

"I'll see if he's in yet."

The sergeant lifted the receiver from a phone base with a bunch of buttons on it, punched in a four-digit number and notified whoever answered that Mr. Rock Wahlman was out in the waiting area. A couple of seconds later, he hung up and instructed Wahlman to push on the solid metal door to his right when the buzzer sounded. Wahlman did that, and then he followed the uniformed officer waiting on the other side down a long hallway to a door that said *HOMICIDE.*

"You can go on in," the officer said. "Detective Collins is in the first office on your left."

"Thanks."

Wahlman pushed the door open and entered the common area of the office suite. There was a young lady sitting at a desk with a computer and a phone and a little sign that said *Tori Moore, Administrative Assistant.* Short brown hair, civilian business attire, stylish eyewear. She didn't look up from the work she was doing when Wahlman walked in. Probably accustomed to the door opening and closing every five minutes. Probably so accustomed to it that she completely tuned it out most of the time.

Wahlman looked around. There was a copy machine and some bookshelves and a long table with a chrome coffeemaker the size of a beer keg on it. Collins was over there filling a ceramic mug that looked like it had been dredged out of the Mississippi.

"Want some coffee?" he asked.

"Does the percolator get washed any more often than the cups?"

Collins laughed. "I brought this in the day I got my gold shield," he said. "These layers of grunge represent nine years of hard work and untold gallons of Hills Brothers."

"You never clean it?"

"Never. And everyone around here knows not to touch it. Help yourself if you want some coffee. It's not bad, especially this time of morning. It starts to get pretty stout after lunch."

Wahlman had been around lawmen long enough to know that many of them developed peculiar little habits along the way. Brown socks on Friday. Whatever. Everyone knew that these idiosyncrasies were supposed to keep bad things from happening, although nobody ever actually said that out loud. You go thousands of days without washing your coffee mug, and you go thousands of days without ending up in the emergency room or the morgue. You know that it's totally irrational to think that there's a correlation between this thing and that thing, but you continue the behavior anyway. Just in case.

Wahlman grabbed a paper cup from a stack on the table. He filled it and took a sip and followed Collins into his office. There was a small wooden desk with a computer and some pictures on it and a steel file cabinet and a corkboard and some chairs, everything crammed into a space about the size of a station wagon.

Wahlman took a seat in one of the wooden chairs in front of the desk, Collins in the padded vinyl one behind it. The desk and both of the wooden chairs had been coated with the same shade of blue that had been used on the exterior of the building. Wahlman figured the paint must have been on sale, or maybe even free.

He took another sip of the coffee.

"This is good," he said.

Collins nodded. "You might need something a little stronger when you hear what I'm going to tell you," he said.

"First of all, our divers didn't find a knife or any other kind of weapon down there in the canal."

"I knew they wouldn't," Wahlman said. "The assault must have taken place a mile or two before the truck went off the highway. No reason for the killer to leave the weapon behind."

"Right. So now I'm wondering how the assailant managed to get out of the truck while it was still moving. It had to have been going sixty or seventy miles an hour. Maybe even faster than that."

"The bridge over Lake Pontchartrain," Wahlman said. "You could jump out of the passenger side of the truck, land in the water and then swim ashore."

"Sure," Collins said. "If you're in a James Bond movie or something. That shit doesn't happen in real life."

"Depends on how desperate you are to get away. I cuffed a sailor to a drainpipe one time while I chased his friend down a fire escape. Two bricks of heroin on the kitchen table. They were breaking it up and weighing it and spooning it into smaller bags for distribution. The guy cuffed to the pipe cut his own hand off with a broken beer bottle. Never did find him or the dope."

"What about the friend?"

"He's doing twenty in Leavenworth. Hard to say which one of them got the worst end of the deal."

"I guess we could check the lake," Collins said. "But I really don't think that's how it happened. Anyway, I wanted to let you know that we identified the victim. What was the name of the orphanage you grew up in?"

"Fine Place West. A misnomer if there ever was one. It was in the western part of Tennessee, so I guess that part made sense. They shut it down a few years ago. What's the vic's name?"

"Darrell Renfro. He also spent some time in an orphanage, but not that one. He was in a place in Illinois for a while, but apparently he was adopted when he was six."

"What was his name before he was adopted?"

"I don't know. The person I talked to said his records were archived years ago. We'll probably have to get a court order if we want to pursue that angle any further. Anyway, you and Renfro look almost exactly alike, and you were both orphans, and your name came up as a possible match when we ran his fingerprints."

"So that's it," Wahlman said. "He's my twin brother."

"Different date of birth, so I don't think he's your twin. But it certainly would appear that the two of you are related. We'll have to run a DNA test to know for sure."

"It blows my mind that we were both on the same stretch of highway the other night, and that I was the one who ended up trying to rescue him. It's either the most bizarre coincidence in history, or someone—"

"Set it up," Collins said, finishing Wahlman's thought for him. "And believe it or not, we discovered something even stranger than all that. We got a second possible match on the prints."

"A second possible match?"

"Guy named Jack Reacher."

"Never heard of him."

"I did a little research," Collins said. "He was an officer in the army. Special Investigations. Served thirteen years. Apparently he was involved in some questionable activities after he got out."

"What kind of questionable activities?"

"Some vigilante stuff. I haven't read through everything, but it seems that for quite a few years he had a habit of showing up in places where trouble was brewing."

Wahlman looked down at his own fingertips, thinking about the day he was sworn in at the United States Armed Forces Processing Station in Memphis, the day his prints were added to the FBI database.

"So I might have two brothers," he said.

"No. Reacher was born in nineteen-sixty."

"So he's—"

"Yeah. A long time ago."

"And he was related to Renfro and me?"

"I don't know. The only thing we can say for sure right now is that the three of you have similar fingerprints. Not identical, but similar enough for the computer to flag them as possible matches. Which is rare. I've been in law enforcement quite a few years, and I've never seen that happen. Fingerprints are usually unique enough for the computer to distinguish one family member from another, even with identical twins."

Wahlman nodded. "Now that you mention it, I remember reading about that one time. Something about various environmental factors in the womb affecting the grooves and ridges. So how is it even possible that Renfro and Reacher and I have prints that are so close to being the same?"

"I don't have an answer for that," Collins said. "I'm just as baffled as you are. We have an expert coming from Baton Rouge to take a look, but it's probably going to be tomorrow before she can make it down here. In the meantime, I have some paperwork I need you to fill out. And a nurse is supposed to stop by in a little while and swab your cheeks for the DNA test."

11

It was almost noon by the time Wahlman made it back out to the parking lot. Allison was sitting there with the windows open, doing some more work on the crossword puzzle she'd started earlier.

"You're not finished with that thing yet?" Wahlman said.

"I took a short nap."

"Must be nice. I had to wait for a nurse to come and jam some cotton-tipped sticks into my mouth. She drew some blood, too."

Wahlman showed her the square of gauze taped to the inside of his left elbow.

"You poor thing," Allison said. "Did she at least give you a lollipop?"

"It was a he," Wahlman said. "And no he didn't. Which is pretty infuriating, now that you mention it. This is the last time I'll ever come *here* for DNA testing."

Allison laughed. Wahlman filled her in on everything he'd learned from talking to Detective Collins.

"Sounds to me like you've found your great-great-grandfather," she said, referring to the man named Jack Reacher.

"Sounds to me like a glitch in the computer system," Wahlman said. "There's no way the three of us really have such similar fingerprints. It just doesn't happen."

"Can't the police examine them the old fashioned way? With a magnifying glass or whatever?"

"They've called in an expert. So we'll see what happens. Right now I need to find out who killed Darrell Renfro and put Walter Babineaux in the hospital. I need to do it before the police find the video of me running away from the sandwich shop, and I need to do it before the same people try to kill me. Again."

Allison started the car, rolled the windows up, switched the air conditioner on.

"Want to go back to the hotel?" she asked.

"I need a gun. Any idea where I can get one?"

"Why would I have an idea about that?"

"Just asking."

"You think I'm some kind of criminal, don't you?"

"Actually, I don't know anything about you," Wahlman said. "Which doesn't seem quite fair, since you know so much about me."

"What do you want to know?"

"I want to know why you need ten thousand dollars by Wednesday."

Allison stared through the windshield. The sunlight reflecting off the dashboard made her eyes glow aquamarine.

"Ask me about something else," she said. "Anything else.

I don't want to talk about that."

"Do you know where I can get a gun?"

Allison sighed. "I know a place," she said. "But I don't want to go there."

"Because it's the same people you owe money to?"

"Yes."

"You can park a block away and stay in the car," Wahlman said. "I'll go in by myself."

"Can't we wait until tomorrow? That way I can go ahead and pay them and be done with it."

"I need a gun today. I want to go to my room at the hotel and fish the business card with Clifford T. Drake's cell phone number on it out of the trash can. The man pretending to be Clifford T. Drake, that is."

"Fake Drake," Allison said.

"Right. I need a gun in case the guys he sent to kill me are watching the room."

"I thought you said you couldn't read the number on the back of that card. I thought you said the ink bled."

"It did. But your comment about a magnifying glass gave me an idea. Maybe the pen left enough of an indentation for me to make out the number."

Allison put the car in gear.

"I can't believe I'm doing this," she said.

She steered out of the police station parking lot, got back on the interstate and took the Pontchartrain Expressway across the river. A few minutes later she exited on Belle Chase Highway, following signs that said *NAVAL AIR STATION, NEW ORLEANS.*

"We're going to the base?" Wahlman asked.

"We're going to an ice cream store in a strip mall. It's not far from NAS."

"I met some guys from one of the squadrons there when I was stationed in Spain. VP Ninety-Four, I think. They were on deployment. They kept telling me I should pick New Orleans for my next duty station."

"But you didn't?"

"I made it my first choice. But the navy doesn't always give you your first choice. They sent me to San Diego."

"I've heard it's nice out there," Allison said.

She turned down a residential street, pulled over to the curb, gave Wahlman directions to the ice cream place. She told him what to say when he got there, and how much money he would need for the purchase. He took three crisp one hundred dollar bills out of his wallet and folded them into one of his back pockets, climbed out of the car and started walking.

The strip mall was about half a mile from where Allison had parked. It was a warm day and Wahlman had worked up a sweat by the time he got there. Hardware, pharmacy, auto parts, grocery. Two vacant storefronts, and then a narrow one in the corner with a pink and white striped awning and a sign that said *DENA JO'S OLD FASHIONED ICE CREAM.*

Business was not booming. Only one vehicle in the designated parking lot, no customers at the tables.

A bell jingled as Wahlman pushed his way through the door and stepped up to the counter. A slender young man wearing a spotless white shirt and a paper hat asked him how he was doing.

"Fine," Wahlman said. "How about you?"

"Great. What can I get for you today?"

"One scoop of almond-raspberry in a cup," Wahlman said.

"Sorry, sir. We're all out of that flavor."

"You don't have any in the back?"

The man gestured toward a door that said EMPLOYEES ONLY.

"See for yourself," he said.

Wahlman opened the door and walked into a room lined with steel storage shelves. It was freezing in there. Literally. Giant cardboard containers had been placed in rows on the shelves, each tubular box labeled with the flavor of ice cream that was inside it. Wahlman counted nineteen different varieties, none of which were almond-raspberry. There was an insulated suit hanging on a hook in the corner. It looked like something you might see on an arctic explorer. Or an astronaut.

Wahlman waited.

And waited.

A digital thermometer hanging from one of the shelves said that it was minus five degrees Fahrenheit in there. Wahlman's teeth were chattering and his fingertips were turning blue. He was about to retreat back to the front of the store when a door on the other side of the room swung open and a man wearing a black leather jacket and a ski mask walked in carrying a briefcase.

"Show me the cash," the man said.

Wahlman pulled the money out of his back pocket and handed it to the man, who smelled strongly of tobacco. The man set the briefcase on the floor, and then he turned around and left the room without saying another word.

Wahlman picked up the briefcase and exited the freezer, nodding to the man in the paper hat as he jingled through the door and made his way out to a very welcome change in temperature.

12

Wahlman didn't open the briefcase until he was back in the car with Allison.

The .38 revolver had cost double what it was worth, but that was the price you paid for convenience.

For not having to wait a week for the paperwork to go through.

"Now all I need are some shells," Wahlman said, spinning the cylinder and viewing the unimpeded daylight beaming through all six of the chambers.

"You're kidding," Allison said. "They didn't put any bullets in the gun?"

Before Wahlman could respond, someone started tapping on the window on Allison's side. Someone with an enormously large belly and a baseball bat.

"Start the car," Wahlman said. "Let's get out of here."

But Allison didn't start the car. She rolled the window down and asked the man standing there what he wanted.

"What do you think I want?" the man said. "I want my money."

"It's not due until tomorrow," Allison said.

The man stepped to the front of the car and smashed the driver side headlight with the baseball bat. He pounded the front fender on that side a couple of times, and then he waddled back over to the window and looked at his watch.

"Tomorrow starts at midnight," he shouted. "About ten hours from now. What difference is ten hours going to make? Either you have the money, or you don't. And since you obviously don't—"

Wahlman climbed out and slammed the door. He walked around to the driver side and inspected the broken headlight and the dents in the fender, told Allison to roll her window up and lock the doors. He was downwind from the man with the bat, and he could smell the odor coming off of his body—a putrid mixture of whiskey and rotting fish guts.

There was a silver SUV with tinted windows parked about twenty feet behind Allison's car. It was the single vehicle that had been parked in the lot at the ice cream place. Wahlman had seen it drive by him a couple of times after he left. At first he was concerned that it might be the people who were trying to kill him. Now he knew it was Tanner. The loan shark. Apparently Tanner had followed him after the transaction at Dena Jo's, maybe suspicious because he was on foot. Maybe suspicious that he was a cop or something. Selling any kind of firearm without a license was a serious offense. Hence the coded language and the long wait in the walk-in freezer. No telling what kind of shady business went on in there. Money laundering came to mind.

Maybe some crystal meth packed in with the mint chocolate chip.

Tanner was about six feet tall and six feet wide. He was one of the fattest people Wahlman had ever seen. He wore yellow pants and a yellow shirt and a black sports jacket that could have doubled as a boat cover. He looked like a gigantic bumble bee.

"Leave her alone," Wahlman said. "She'll have your money for you tomorrow afternoon. I guarantee it."

"Where's my briefcase?" Tanner asked.

"That's why you followed me?"

"You were supposed to put it in the trash can by the hardware store."

Allison rolled her window down and handed the briefcase to Wahlman, who then whizzed it toward Tanner like some kind of aerodynamically-challenged Frisbee. It landed on the gritty pavement, skidded and came to a rest at Tanner's feet.

"There you go," Wahlman said. "Hope the asphalt didn't scar it up too bad."

"You should probably get back in the car," Tanner said, tapping the head of the baseball bat against the palm of his hand. "As of now, this is none of your business."

"Allison's my friend," Wahlman said. "So I'm making it my business."

Tanner laughed. "Well, it's nice to have friends, isn't it? Especially ones as loyal as you seem to be. I have friends, too. And believe me, mine are *incredibly* loyal."

Two guys climbed out of the SUV. They walked up to

where Tanner was standing. One of them was a little taller than Tanner, the other a little shorter. Both of them had square jaws and broad shoulders and thick corded necks. They wore tailored black suits and black ties and white shirts. Military buzz cuts, wraparound shades. Goon A and Goon B, Wahlman thought. From central casting. They didn't say anything. They just stood there with their hands behind their backs.

"I need the money now," Tanner said. "She's already way behind, and she hasn't returned any of my phone calls. I'm a reasonable man, but—"

"You got shit in your ears?" Wahlman asked. "You'll get your money tomorrow. Now tell your guys to get back in the truck before they break a nail or something."

Goon A took a few steps forward.

Goon B followed.

Now they were standing several feet in front of Tanner. Several feet closer to Wahlman. They didn't have their hands behind their backs anymore. They had them at their sides.

And Wahlman could see that each of them was wearing a set of brass knuckles.

"The only thing we're going to break is your face," Goon A said.

"You need to get back in your vehicle," Wahlman said. "Your fat boss might have a heart attack if he has to carry you over there."

Goon A took another step forward, reared back and took a roundhouse swing, aiming for the left side of Wahlman's jaw.

Wahlman had never been hit with brass knuckles before, but he knew what kind of damage they could do. He'd seen an x-ray one time. Sailor in a bar fight up in Philadelphia. The guy's skull had been cracked like an egg.

The roundhouse from Goon A came fast and hard. Wahlman ducked, felt the cold metal graze his left ear, went down dizzily and caught himself with his palm and jammed the sole of his foot into the center of Goon A's knee. He struck the joint squarely, the ligaments snapping like dry twigs as the newly-ruined extremity crumpled in the wrong direction.

Goon A screamed and fell to the pavement while Goon B moved in and kicked Wahlman in the back of his ribcage. Viciously. Repeatedly. Arcing back and following through, swinging the boot like the weight on a pendulum, again and again and again, heaving and grunting, snarling and snorting, pouring everything he had into a stupid slobbering anger-fueled frenzy that left his incredibly loyal ass almost totally exhausted after about thirty seconds.

Wahlman knew that his back would be extremely sore tomorrow, but he also knew that Goon B hadn't done any lasting damage. He hadn't broken any ribs. The latissimus dorsi muscles on Wahlman's back were much thicker than most people's. This was partly due to some of the exercises he did when he played football, but it was mostly due to genetics. By the time Wahlman turned fifteen years old, his body looked like something out of a comic book. Pecs like blocks of concrete, biceps the size of cantaloupes. All without lifting a single dumbbell. Everyone assumed that he spent a lot of time at the gym, but he didn't. It was just the way he was built. The massive layers of muscle tissue provided him with great strength, and they also protected his bones and internal organs against the kind of blunt trauma Goon B had been delivering so enthusiastically over the past half-minute or so.

Wahlman was still lightheaded from being clipped with the brass knuckles, but he could tell that Goon B was getting tired. He could tell that the intensity of the impacts had started to wane. As Tanner edged a little closer to the ruckus, Wahlman rolled over and grabbed the boot Goon B had been kicking him with and twisted it clockwise. Goon B lost his balance, fell and landed right on top of Goon A, and—based on the guttural string of shrieks and expletives that ensued—reignited the pain in the part of his leg that had once been a knee.

Wahlman didn't wait for Goon B to get up. He was on him in an instant. He grabbed his skinny black tie and yanked upward on it, causing his chest to rise and his head to tilt back, and causing another series of agonized cries from Goon A, who now had two people on top of him. When Goon B instinctively straightened his neck in an effort to correct the awkward and uncomfortable position, Wahlman met him with an elbow to the nose. There was a sickening crunch and a shower of bright red blood and some coughing and gurgling, followed by a sudden unsettling silence as both of the injured men apparently lost consciousness.

Tanner took a step backward, toward the SUV. He still had the bat, but he wasn't holding it in a threatening manner anymore.

"This isn't over," he said.

"Looks over to me," Wahlman said.

"I'm going to get my money, one way or another."

"You'll get it tomorrow. Like I told you before. Minus whatever the damage to Allison's car adds up to. Right now you should probably get in your truck and call whoever you need to call to come and scrape these unfortunate gentlemen off the asphalt."

"I could have busted your head open with this bat," Tanner said.

"And I could have shoved that bat up your ass," Wahlman said. "Sideways."

Tanner turned around and started walking toward the SUV.

Wahlman walked around to the passenger side of Allison's car and climbed back into the front seat.

"I guess I forgot to tell you to put the briefcase in the trash can," Allison said.

"Yeah," Wahlman said. "I guess you did."

13

A box of .38 shells purchased legally at a sporting goods store cost almost as much as the revolver had cost in the freezer over at Dena Jo's. Wahlman didn't need a whole box of bullets, but you couldn't just walk in and ask for half a dozen. It didn't work that way. You had to buy the entire sealed box and you had to sign for it and you had to pay the tax. You could buy single rounds on the black market, but Wahlman didn't have any of those kinds of connections in New Orleans.

Tanner was the only person Allison knew who sometimes dealt in undocumented merchandise, but of course he wouldn't have sold Wahlman a water pistol after the incident over on the West Bank.

So Wahlman had to buy the entire box of .38 caliber cartridges, and he had to pay a lot of money for it. Not to mention that by law every such transaction had to be conducted in front of a video camera, which meant that the police could eventually obtain even more incriminating evidence to use against Wahlman if they picked him up for the sandwich shop shooting. Which they would, eventually, unless he found the real shooters first.

Allison parked her car in the hotel's garage. Wahlman broke the seal on the box of bullets and started loading the gun.

"Sorry about all the trouble," Allison said.

"Me too. But I feel better now that I have a weapon and some ammunition."

Allison started massaging her temples with her fingertips.

"I'm glad someone feels better," she said.

"You have a headache?"

"I'll be okay. I have some pills in my carryon bag. Are you going to your room now?"

"My truck is parked somewhere in this garage. I'm going to try to find it so I can get my luggage. Then I'll go to my room and take a look at the business card with the cell phone number on it. Then I'll come to your room and try to call the guy."

"Don't you think the maids have emptied your trash cans by now?"

"I left the *DO NOT DISTURB* sign on the door," Wahlman said. "So the room should be just as I left it."

"Okay. Is there anything I can do to help you right now?"

"Just go to your room and wait. I'll be there in a little while."

Wahlman stuffed some extra shells into the right front pocket of his jeans, climbed out and slid the revolver into his waistband and walked around the garage until he found his truck, careful to stay in the shadows until he was relatively certain there weren't any assassins in the vicinity.

Level 5, Section H, Space 14. Right where it was supposed to be, right where his valet parking receipt said it would be. He hadn't wanted Allison to drive him there, because he didn't want her to know where the vehicle was parked. She seemed to be all right, but he had been hurt more than once by people who seemed to be all right. There was only one person in the world he fully trusted, and Allison Bentley wasn't that person. Especially since the goof-up with the briefcase. Wahlman believed that it had been unintentional, but still. Those were the kinds of mistakes that got people killed.

Wahlman's suitcase was in the back, zippered into a weatherproof vinyl cover. He pulled it out and carried it to the elevator, and then he decided that the stairs might be safer. He walked down to the first level and out to the street and around to the hotel.

He climbed the stairs to the fourth floor, went to his room and promptly discovered that his key didn't work anymore. It had worked just minutes ago when he'd entered the hotel through the side door, but it wasn't working now. He tried the card several times, kept getting the red LED on the electronic indicator at the front of the slot.

He looked around, saw a housekeeping cart outside a room down at the end of the hallway. He walked down there and asked the woman pulling sheets off the bed if she could let him into his room.

"Which room?" she asked.

"Four sixty-two. I have my key, but it's not working for

some reason."

The woman looked at her clipboard. "Says here that room's vacant. I was going to clean it after I clean this one."

"It's not vacant," Wahlman said. "It's my room. I don't want it cleaned right now."

"I'll have to get with my supervisor on that," the woman said.

Wahlman nodded. The elevator bank was right around the corner and his suitcase was heavy and he was tired of taking the stairs. He made it down to the first floor, trotted over to the front desk, waited for a man wearing an off-white linen suit and an off-white straw fedora to ask a million or so questions before deciding on a double with two queens, and then he stepped up to the counter and asked the guy standing behind it why he couldn't get into his room. The guy did his thing on the computer, and then he told Wahlman that the account that he had used to check in with did not contain sufficient funds to cover the hotel's standard hold on incidental charges.

"That's impossible," Wahlman said. "I have over seven thousand dollars in that account."

"Not according to the statement we received from your bank," the clerk said. "If you would like to provide an alternate form of payment, I would be happy to—"

"Use this," Wahlman said, sliding his Visa card across the desk.

Wahlman didn't like to buy things on credit. He believed in paying as he went. He'd opened the account as an emergency backup, kept a zero balance and a low limit.

He reckoned this qualified as an emergency.

The clerk ran the card and handed over a fresh set of room keys, apologized for the inconvenience and told Wahlman to have a great day.

By the time Wahlman made it back up to his room, the *DO NOT DISTURB* sign on his door handle was gone and the housekeeping cart was nowhere in sight. He opened the door and walked in and saw that the bed had been made and the trash had been emptied.

He set his suitcase down, stepped over to the phone and called the front desk.

"May I help you?"

"I need my garbage back," Wahlman said.

"Excuse me?"

"Would it be possible for me to speak to the housekeeping supervisor?"

"I'll try to transfer you. Hold on just a second."

Wahlman held on for way more than a second. More like two minutes. Finally, the jazzy rendition of a twentieth century song Wahlman couldn't remember the name of stopped abruptly and was replaced by the voice of a man who sounded as though he might have just gotten up from a nap.

"Housekeeping," the man said.

"This is Rock Wahlman in four sixty-two. My trash was emptied a while ago, and I need it back."

"You need your trash back?"

"I accidentally threw something away. A business card. It has a very important phone number on it. I need to get it back."

There was a long pause.

"That's going to be a problem," the man said. "All the trash gets loaded into big plastic bags, and then it's dropped down a chute that empties into a bin in the basement. It's not separated by which room it came from, or even which floor. We're talking half a ton of garbage every day. There's no way you're going to find a business card in that mess."

"I need to try," Wahlman said.

"I can't let you crawl around in that bin. It's not safe. Broken glass, razor blades. Who knows what might be in there. You know what I'm saying?"

"Sure. I know what you're saying. I guess I'll just have to forget about finding that card. I guess it's gone forever. Thanks anyway."

"Sorry I couldn't be of more help."

Wahlman thanked the man again, hung the phone up, walked downstairs and out the side door, headed up to Canal Street to buy some goggles and rubber gloves.

And a magnifying glass, which he'd somehow forgotten to stop for on the way back to the hotel with Allison.

14

It wasn't quite as difficult as the housekeeping supervisor had thought it would be for Wahlman to determine which of the big white plastic bags contained the trash from his room. It only took him about five minutes to find the bag from the fourth floor. The plastic was translucent, and he could see the logo on the box from the chicken place Allison had gone to last night to get their dinner.

He tore the bag open and started ferreting through the nastiness. No broken glass or razor blades, but plenty of stuff that probably should have been sealed into a container with a biohazard stamp on it. There was a dirty diaper that probably should have been sealed in lead and buried deeply in the ground. Half-eaten hamburgers, dental floss, candy wrappers. Someone had discarded a sizeable wedge of birthday cake. Chocolate with chocolate frosting. It said *PY BIR*, and below that, *JA*. Maybe the person's name was Jane. Or Jason. Or Jack. With the hefty tax on sugar these days, Wahlman wondered why so much of the cake had been thrown away. He didn't wonder about it long, though, because right underneath the circular piece of cardboard it had been mounted on was the business card he was looking for.

He reached down and picked up the card, slid it into his back pocket, climbed out of the bin and brushed himself off. He tossed the goggles and the rubber gloves and took the stairs back up to the fourth floor and went to his room.

The clothes he was wearing were filthy from fighting in the street and digging in the trash. He opened his suitcase and set out some clean things—Levi's and socks and boxers and an undershirt, and a blue oxford button-down with tails that could be left out to conceal the revolver—and then he shaved and took a shower and transferred everything from the pockets of his dirty clothes to the pockets of his fresh clothes and made a pot of coffee and looked at the business card with the magnifying glass. He'd used a ballpoint pen to write Fake Drake's number on the card, and the pressure from the point had indeed left an impression, albeit a very faint one. He could make out every number except the second to the last.

The phone started ringing. The only person Wahlman wanted to talk to right now was Allison, and there was no way to be certain that she was the one calling. So instead of answering the phone, Wahlman turned the coffee pot off, stuffed the clothes he'd been wearing earlier into the trash can, slid the .38 into his waistband, zipped up his suitcase and left the room.

As he made his way down the corridor, it occurred to him that maybe he didn't even need his own hotel room anymore. Now that he'd gotten the business card back, the room wasn't much more than a liability. He'd initially hoped to use it as a lure for the assassins, but now he was concerned that the detectives investigating the shooting at the sandwich shop would show up first.

He knocked on Allison's door. She opened it and let him in. The drapes had been closed, and all the lights were off except for the shaded lamp on the nightstand.

"Why is it so dark in here?" Wahlman asked.

"I told you I have a headache," Allison said.

"Did you take something?"

"I did. But it hasn't kicked in yet."

"I need to borrow your cell phone," Wahlman said.

"Did you find the card?"

Wahlman nodded. He pulled the crumpled and stained business card out of his pocket and handed it to her, along with the magnifying glass.

"See if you can make out the second to the last number," he said. "In the meantime, there's another call I need to make."

Wahlman actually needed to make two other calls before he tried Fake Drake. One to the front desk to check out of his room, and one to his bank to see why the hotel had rejected his debit card.

Allison handed him her cell phone, and then she walked over to the nightstand to examine the business card under the lamp.

Wahlman punched in the number for the front desk.

"Guest services. May I help you?"

"This is Rock Wahlman, four sixty-two. I've decided not to take the room after all."

"Is there a problem, sir?"

"There's no problem with the room. I have some urgent business back home, and I'm going to have to leave town sooner than expected."

"So you want to check out right now?"

"Yes."

"You realize that your card will be charged for the full—"

"I know," Wahlman said. "That's fine. Just go ahead and close everything out."

There was a pause and a flurry of keyboard clicks, and then the clerk cheerfully informed Wahlman that he had been checked out of the room and to please visit again soon and to have a nice day.

Wahlman disconnected and punched in the 800 number for his bank. A robot asked him for his account number and personal identification number and gave him a list of things he could do over the phone, including the option to hold for a period of time that might exceed thirty minutes in order to speak to a real live human being.

Wahlman didn't feel like waiting. He felt like slamming the phone down on the floor and stomping it into a million pieces.

Allison must have sensed his frustration.

"What's wrong?" she asked.

"They want me to stand here with my thumb up my ass for half an hour. This is why I usually do all my banking in person."

"If you want, I can put it on speakerphone while you wait."

He walked over to where she was standing and handed her the phone. She tapped the display screen a couple of times, activating a built-in stereo speaker system that you probably could have carried around on a dime. This time, Wahlman remembered the name of the song playing, a country blues number called "A Tomorrow Like Yesterday." It was one of his favorites.

"Thanks," he said. "Were you able to make out that second-to-the-last digit on the back of the business card?"

"I think it's a two. But I'm not sure. Anyway, there are only ten possibilities. You can try one at a time until the guy you want to talk to picks up."

"Fake Drake."

"Yes. Fake Drake. You can use my room phone if you want to."

"I'm afraid the hotel will show up on his caller ID. I went ahead and checked out of my room, by the way. So I'll need to stay here again tonight."

"Okay. Why are you calling your bank?"

"There was a problem with my debit card. Don't worry. I'll get it straightened out."

"You're still going to be able to pay me tomorrow, right?"

"I hope so."

"What do you mean you hope so? You saw the kind of people I'm dealing with. I have to have that money."

"What were you planning to do before I made the offer to pay you?" Wahlman asked.

"Beg for more time. But after what happened a while ago—"

"Tanner's not going to give you more time. Does he know where you're staying?"

"I don't think so."

"Good. Anyway, there's no reason to start panicking yet. I should be able to give you the money tomorrow. Then you can pay Tanner and be done with him."

"That's what I thought was going to happen," Allison said. "Now I'm getting nervous again."

The music coming from the phone stopped abruptly, replaced by a woman who apologized for the wait. She identified herself as Brenda and asked how she could be of assistance today.

Allison tapped the speakerphone off, picked up the device and handed it to Wahlman.

He put it to his ear.

"I had some trouble with my debit card a while ago," he said.

"What kind of trouble?"

"Insufficient funds. Which doesn't make sense, because I know for a fact that there's plenty of money in the account."

"What's your account number?"

Wahlman gave her the number, and a few seconds later she told him his balance.

"That's not right," Wahlman said. "It's off by about seven thousand dollars."

"I'm showing an online transfer of exactly seven

thousand dollars at five-fourteen this morning."

"Transfer to where?"

"Looks like a business account. It's at another bank."

"I never authorized a transfer," Wahlman said. "Someone stole my money."

"The only way that's possible is if they knew your user name and password and the answers to your security questions. Do you know of anyone who might have had access to that information?"

Wahlman did in fact know of someone who had access to that information. Mike Chilton. His best friend. The one person in the world he trusted unequivocally. House keys, passwords, insurance policies. He and Mike Chilton had each other's back on all that stuff.

Wahlman was still concerned about the money, but more than anything he was concerned about Mike. His immediate thought was that Fake Drake had gotten to him somehow.

"I'm going to have to call you back," Wahlman said.

"That's fine," Brenda said. "I'll be here until nine tonight."

She gave Wahlman her personal extension, told him that he still might have to wait on hold for a while, but that at least he wouldn't be routed to a different representative.

"Thanks," Wahlman said.

He disconnected and immediately tried to call Mike Chilton.

No answer.

He left a message, clicked off and handed the phone to Allison. She set it on the nightstand and plugged it into its charger.

"What's going on?" she asked.

"I need to go to Florida," he said.

"Why?"

"Someone transferred most of the money out of my account. I need to find out about that, and I need to make sure my friend Mike is okay."

"Why would your friend Mike not be okay?"

"He's the only person besides me who knows my password. I'm afraid—"

"Maybe someone hacked into the account," Allison said.

"It's possible. And Mike does have a habit of turning his phone off sometimes, so I'm not ready to go into panic mode just yet. Whatever the case, I need to go home and straighten everything out."

"Where in Florida do you live?"

Wahlman told her the name of the town.

"It's inland," he said. "Between Jacksonville and Gainesville."

"How far is that from here?"

"About ten hours."

"What about me?"

"I was thinking you might want to come with me."

Allison glanced toward the window. She took a deep breath.

"Will we be back by tomorrow?" she asked.

"I don't see how."

"I need to give Tanner that money tomorrow."

"He might have to wait another day or two. Go ahead

and get your stuff together. I'm going to walk downstairs and use one of the desktops to change my password."

Wahlman left the room and took the stairs down to the first floor. While he was down there, he used the payphone to call Detective Collins. He wanted to let him know he was leaving New Orleans for a couple of days, and he wanted to give him Allison's cell phone number in case there were any new developments he needed to know about.

He was especially interested in the results of the DNA tests. With recent advances in processing, preliminary results were usually available within twenty-four hours, and Wahlman was anxious to find out how he and Darrell Renfro—and Jack Reacher—were related.

15

Collins wasn't in, so Wahlman left a message with the administrative assistant there in the office suite. The one with the short brown hair and the stylish glasses. Tori something or another.

"I'll be sure he gets the message," she said.

"Thanks," Wahlman said.

"No problem. Have a good one."

Wahlman disconnected, took the stairs back up to the fourth floor. As he approached Allison's room, he noticed that the door was ajar. Not much, just a crack. Just a razor-thin slit, but enough to allow a wedge of light to spill out into the hallway, enough to subtly announce that the door had not been properly secured.

Wahlman knew for a fact that he hadn't left it that way.

And he was fairly certain that Allison wouldn't have left it that way.

Which meant that there was a good possibility that someone else had been in the room.

Or that someone else was still in the room.

There was no way for Wahlman to know for sure who the *someone else* was, but three distinct possibilities immediately came to mind: NOPD detectives investigating the shooting at the sandwich shop, in which case Allison was probably very nervous but still physically okay; some more of Tanner's hired muscle, in which case Allison was *definitely* very nervous and maybe *not* physically okay; assassins sent by Fake Drake, in which case Allison was dead.

Wahlman pulled the .38 from his waistband, tiptoed to the threshold, leaned in and cupped his free hand against the painted steel door, hoping to hear the calm and reasonable voices of police detectives out searching for potential witnesses.

Nothing.

Total silence.

Which meant that it wasn't the cops. If it had been the cops, there would have been voices. Cops don't hang around when there's nothing left to say. Not in Wahlman's experience. When there's nothing left to say, cops leave. Every time. No exceptions.

Which narrowed the distinct possibilities down to two: Tanner's guys, or Fake Drake's guys.

Wahlman stepped back and pushed the door open a few inches with his finger.

"Allison. You in there?"

Nothing.

Total silence.

And then a click. Metallic. Like maybe a switchblade opening or a pair of handcuffs locking, or the hammer of a pistol being pulled back.

Wahlman pushed the door all the way open with his foot, walked into the room with his arms outstretched, both hands wrapped tightly around the grips of the revolver, sweeping left and then right and then left again, sweeping past the drapes and the bed and the long wooden unit that served as a desk and a dresser and a TV stand, sweeping past the framed prints bolted to the walls and the vanity and the mirror in the little alcove that led to the bathroom, unable to determine the origin of the click, seeing nothing out of the ordinary except that Allison wasn't there.

Unless she was in the bathroom.

Wahlman walked to the alcove and knocked on the door.

"Rock? Is that you?"

A sense of relief washed over Wahlman like a warm breeze.

"Why was your door open?" he asked.

"My door was open?"

"Yeah. So instead of *me* moseying on in, it could have been—"

"I can barely hear you. I'll be out in a minute."

Wahlman slid the gun back into his waistband, walked over to the bed and sat down. Then he noticed that the door to the room was still open, so he got up and closed it. Remembering that there were still a couple of beers in the refrigerator, he walked over there and got one out and twisted the cap off and chugged about half of it on his way back to the bed. He sat down again and grabbed Allison's cell phone from the nightstand and tried to call Mike

Chilton. Still no answer.

Allison walked out of the bathroom with a towel around her head.

"I figured you'd be ready to go by now," Wahlman said.

"I've been feeling kind of icky since this morning, when I had to sit out in the car all that time. I thought I better take a shower before we hit the road."

"How's your headache?"

"Better. Thanks."

"Why was your door open?"

"I don't know. You must not have closed it all the way when you left the room a while ago."

"I closed it all the way."

"You're sure about that?"

"Yes."

"Then I don't know. Maybe the maid came by while I was in the—"

Before Allison was able to finish her sentence, before she was able to say *shower*, the drapes parted and a man with a sound-suppressed semiautomatic pistol stepped forward and drilled two rounds into her chest.

Wahlman rolled off the bed and hit the floor a split second before two more bullets thudded into the mattress. He grabbed the revolver from his waistband and raised it over the edge of the bed like a periscope and started firing in the general direction of the assailant, the reports from the .38 booming out like cannon fire in the enclosed space. Wahlman squeezed off all six rounds, reached into his pocket and pulled out a handful of shells, thinking it was useless, almost certain that he was going to die before he had a chance to reload, but doing it anyway, because there was no point in not doing it, no point in just lying there and waiting for the assassin to step around the corner of the bed and finish him off.

Wahlman pushed the cartridges into the chambers one-by-one, his heart thumping like a boxer on a speed bag. He managed to load all six of the bullets, and then he waited and wondered why he wasn't dead yet. A few seconds ticked by, and then a few more, and then Wahlman leaned up and peaked over the top of the mattress and saw that the bad guy was on the floor next to Allison and that the top of his skull was missing.

Wahlman stood and walked over to Allison and checked her for a pulse, knowing just by looking at her that she didn't have one but checking anyway, also knowing that the six shots he'd fired had made a lot of noise and that he needed to get out of there in a hurry.

He took a deep breath, trying to think everything through, trying not to panic. The digital clock on the nightstand said 2:47. Which meant that there probably weren't many people around. Especially on a Monday. The weekend crowd was long gone and the housekeeping associates had finished with their cleaning duties and the people checking in for the night weren't in their rooms yet. The tourists in town for the week were out and about doing touristy things, and the business people were out and about pitching their crummy little products that nobody needed or sitting around bored out of their minds in a meeting somewhere or out doing whatever else those kinds of people did all day. The rooms seemed to be pretty well insulated, so it was possible nobody had noticed the six earsplitting shots from Wahlman's gun.

Possible, but there was no point in sticking around to find out.

Wahlman grabbed Allison's cell phone and charging cable and the business card with Fake Drake's number on it from the nightstand and jammed it all into his pocket. He kicked the pistol away from the bad guy's hand, bent over and picked it up and wiped the blood off with some tissues from the little chrome dispenser on the front of the vanity. He unzipped his suitcase and tossed the pistol in there and zipped it back up and grabbed it by the handle and walked to the door. He looked out the peephole, and then he opened the door and stepped out into the hallway and headed for the stairs.

16

It was almost two o'clock Tuesday morning by the time Wahlman made it to his house in Florida. He usually referred to the little place as a *cabin*, which he thought sounded marginally better than *shack*. Five hundred square feet, board-and-batten siding, metal roof. There was one small bedroom and a small living room and a small kitchen, and a bathroom with an enormous cast iron claw foot tub that was probably two hundred years old and probably weighed five hundred pounds. The exterior was situated so that the back of the house faced the road. There was no back door, but there was a window on the back side of the house, and Wahlman could see that the kitchen light he'd left on was still on.

He stopped and got his mail out of the box, steered into the gravel driveway and around to the wooden deck in front. Switched the engine off and the headlights and sat there for a while and stared down the slope toward the lake, which was glistening calmly in the moonlight.

For ten and a half hours he'd been wondering why the

assailant had waited for Allison to come out of the bathroom before he attacked. At first Wahlman thought the guy must have been one of Fake Drake's hit men, maybe part of the same team that had tried to kill him at the sandwich shop, maybe part of the same team that had been successful in killing Darrell Renfro out on I-10. But if that was the case, the way it went down didn't make much sense. Why didn't the assassin step out from behind the drapes and finish his business as soon as Wahlman walked into the room?

So maybe it wasn't one of Fake Drake's guys after all. Maybe it was one of Tanner's guys, out for revenge. But that didn't make much sense either. Why kill Allison? Why kill someone who owes you money? Seemed like a good way to never get paid.

After turning it over in his mind a thousand times, it seemed to Wahlman that he should be the one lying in a puddle of blood on the hotel room floor right now and that Allison should be the one still breathing. That was the way it seemed, but of course that wasn't the way it was.

He decided not to think about it anymore right now. He was exhausted. He needed sleep. Maybe he would be able to think a little more clearly in the morning.

He got out of the truck and grabbed his suitcase from the back, climbed the four wooden steps and crossed the deck, unlocked the nice set of French doors he'd installed two years ago and walked inside. The cabin had that strange feel to it that all houses have after you've been away for a while, quiet and still and kind of foreign.

Wahlman set his suitcase down and turned some lights

on. There was a loveseat in the living room and a wingback chair and a small folding table that you could put your drink on while you were watching television. Pine planks overhead, exposed beams and a ceiling fan that wasn't much to look at but helped move the air around, helped with the heating and air conditioning costs, which were minimal in such a small space anyway but every little bit helped.

Wahlman had driven by Mike Chilton's place on the way home, hoping that Mike might still be up, hoping to find out why he wasn't answering his phone. It was late and the house was dark and he knew that Mike might be asleep, but he'd walked up on the porch and knocked anyway. Mike never came to the door. Which didn't necessarily mean that anything was wrong, because Mike was the soundest sleeper Wahlman had ever known. The shrillest of alarm clocks were of no use to him, and he'd even slept through a hurricane one time. You pretty much had to grab him and shake him to wake him up. So Wahlman wasn't terribly worried that he hadn't answered the door. His car had been in the garage and the house had looked okay. No mail in the mailbox, no circulars littering the driveway. Wahlman had driven away, planning to check again in the morning but figuring that Mike was just being Mike.

Wahlman walked to the bathroom, peeled his clothes off and took a long hot shower. He put on a fresh pair of boxer shorts and nothing else and went into the kitchen and made a peanut butter sandwich and opened a bottle of beer. He sat down and looked at his mail. Phone bill, electric bill, a credit card offer, sales papers from some of the local stores.

And a letter from Clifford T. Drake, Attorney at Law.

Fake Drake.

Wahlman hadn't tried the number on the business card yet. He hadn't wanted to mess with it while he was driving, because there was still a digit he was unsure of.

He tore the envelope open and read the letter, which was nothing formal, just a handwritten note.

Dear Mr. Wahlman,

I'm sorry you were unable to make it to our appointment Sunday afternoon. I've tried calling several times, but there was no answer. Please call me at your earliest convenience.

Thanks,
C.T. Drake

There was a phone number at the bottom of the note. Wahlman checked it against the one on the business card. It was the same. Allison had been correct. The illegible digit on the business card had been a two.

Wahlman used Allison's phone to make the call.

Four rings, and then a sleepy male voice picked up and grunted hello.

"This is Wahlman."

Silence for a beat.

"Where are you?" the male voice asked, sounding a little perkier now, undoubtedly noticing the incoming area code and thinking the call had originated in New Orleans.

"It's none of your business where I am," Wahlman said.

"You sound angry. If anyone should be angry, it should be me. Do you have any idea what time it is?"

"This was my earliest convenience."

"I see. Well, if you wouldn't mind—"

"Why did you kill Darrell Renfro? Why are you trying to kill me?"

"What?"

"A woman named Allison Bentley is dead now too. I guess you're going to tell me you don't know anything about that either. I guess you're going to stick with your story about the inheritance. I did a little research. Once upon a time there was indeed a lawyer in New Orleans named Clifford T. Drake. He even specialized in estate planning. But—"

"He was my father," the male voice said. "My full name is Clifford Terrence Drake Junior."

"You're lying," Wahlman said. "There was no mention of a son in the obituary."

"My father and I had a falling out about ten years ago. He sort of disowned me. Cut me out of his will, the whole nine yards. I can tell that you're really upset, Mr. Wahlman, but I can promise you I had nothing to do with the things you're talking about."

"How do I know you're telling the truth?"

"Well, you could check my Louisiana Bar credentials. It's all a matter of public record."

"Maybe I'll do that," Wahlman said.

"Good. Call me back in the morning and we'll talk some more."

The man claiming to be Clifford Terrence Drake Junior hung up without saying another word.

Wahlman set the phone down, ate the rest of his sandwich and drank the rest of his beer. He put his dishes in the sink and walked to the bathroom and brushed his teeth, and when he finished he stood there and looked at his reflection in the mirror.

"That guy's full of shit," he said, staring into his own tired eyes. "Even if his name really is Clifford Terrence Drake Junior, and even if he really is an estate attorney, and even if his office really is under renovation. Even if all that's true, it doesn't mean that he's not responsible for what happened on the interstate and in the sandwich shop and in Allison's hotel room. Right? Because someone's definitely trying to kill me. There's no doubt about that. Someone who knew exactly where I was supposed to be Sunday afternoon and exactly when I was supposed to be there. It had to be Drake. It had to be. The only other person who knew about that meeting was Mike Chilton. So it had to be Drake, right?"

Wahlman's reflection said nothing.

17

Wahlman woke up at the usual time Tuesday morning.

5:27.

Which meant that he'd only slept about two hours. Which meant that he should have been dragging ass. But he wasn't. He felt energized, ready to go. Only not in a good way. More like a mechanical toy that had been wound too tightly, torqued to the breaking point and then pointed toward the edge of a table.

He couldn't find a clean pair of jeans, so he put on the same pair he'd worn yesterday, along with a white t-shirt and a striped button-down. He drank a pot of coffee and watched some news on television, and then he grabbed Mike Chilton's spare set of keys and left the cabin.

Mike lived in a nice big house on the other side of the lake. He'd done well for himself after the navy, finishing his master's degree and starting a software consultant company. He spent sixteen hours a day in his office sometimes, seven days a week sometimes, but he always said he enjoyed the work, and he certainly was raking in the dough. Wahlman wasn't jealous of Mike's success. Not even a little bit. Mike was his best friend, and he was happy for him.

Wahlman steered into Mike's driveway, cut the engine and climbed out of the truck and mounted the porch and knocked on the front door.

No answer.

It was a little after nine, and Mike was usually up by eight. His car was still in the garage, so it didn't seem likely that he'd gone anywhere.

Of course it was possible that he was still in bed.

Wahlman didn't usually enter Mike's house without being invited, but the intrusion seemed warranted under the circumstances. He slid the key into the deadbolt and opened the door and stepped into the foyer. To his right there was a set of stairs that led to the bedrooms on the second floor. He shouted Mike's name, waited a few seconds, climbed the stairs and walked to the master bedroom. As he reached to open the door, Allison's cell phone trilled.

Wahlman looked at the display, saw that it was Detective Collins.

Collins.

With everything else that had happened over the past twenty-four hours, Wahlman had kind of pushed Collins to the back of his mind. He pretty much knew what was coming, knew that it wasn't going to be good, but he figured there was no escaping it now. Best to just go ahead and deal with it.

He tapped the screen and answered the call.

"This is Wahlman," he said.

"Collins, NOPD Homicide. I need you to come to the station as soon as possible."

"I drove home," Wahlman said. "I'm in Florida."

Collins sighed. "There was a double homicide in the hotel you were staying at," he said. "A man and a woman. The coroner thinks two different guns were used, neither of which were found on the premises. The cell phone you're talking on is registered to the woman."

"You guys work fast," Wahlman said.

"I need you to come to the station."

"I didn't shoot her."

Collins sighed some more. "I also received some footage from a security camera this morning," he said. "It shows you exiting the back door of the sandwich shop across from the hotel, and it shows you running up the alley toward Canal Street. This was right around the time the owner of the restaurant was shot. Man named Walter Babineaux."

"I didn't shoot him either."

"I want to believe you, Wahlman. I don't think you had anything to do with Darrell Renfro out there on the interstate, and I want to believe you didn't have anything to do with Babineaux in the sandwich shop or the man and the woman in the hotel. I want to believe you, but—"

"Is Babineaux still alive?"

"Last I heard."

"Is he conscious? Has anyone talked to him yet?"

"I'm not going to sugarcoat this," Collins said, ignoring Wahlman's questions. "We have a warrant for your arrest. Assault with intent to kill. We're working on a second warrant, and that one's going to be for first degree murder. I need you to drive to the nearest sheriff's department substation and turn yourself in. They'll get the extradition process started, get you transferred back to New Orleans before the end of the week. Otherwise, we're going to have to initiate a—"

"Who do you think I murdered?" Wahlman asked.

"The woman in the hotel room. The man too. But you have the woman's phone, so it's going to be—"

"Her name's Allison."

"Right. So you knew her. I can go ahead and take a confession over the phone if—"

"I didn't kill her," Wahlman said. "I killed the man, but not Allison. It was self-defense. He shot her, and then he started shooting at me. I know the scene is still fresh, but eventually you're going to find two nine millimeter rounds in the mattress, and six thirty-eights elsewhere. One of the thirty-eights just happened to plow through the top of the guy's head."

"We're going to sort it all out when you get back to New Orleans."

"I'm not turning myself in," Wahlman said. "Not yet."

"You have to. The warrant's out there. You're a fugitive. You're considered armed and dangerous. Every law enforcement officer in the country is going to know what you look like in a matter of hours. There's nowhere to hide. Might as well make it easy on yourself."

Wahlman took a deep breath. "Did you get the DNA results back yet?" he asked.

"Irrelevant."

"But did you?"

"Yeah. But something's wrong. We're going to have to redo the whole thing."

"Some sort of mistake in the lab?"

"Had to be," Collins said. "Because according to the results, you and Darrell Renfro and Jack Reacher are all the same person."

"What does that even mean?"

"We'll talk about it when you get to New Orleans. Right now you need to drive to the substation and turn yourself in."

"I can't do that."

"Then you're in for a world of trouble, my friend."

"Talk to Babineaux," Wahlman said.

And then he hung up.

He figured it was a good time to get rid of Allison's cell phone. The whole lack of privacy thing was one of the reasons he didn't own one. He didn't like the fact that anyone with a computer could track his whereabouts twenty-four hours a day. The only reason he'd taken the phone in the first place was so he could keep trying to call Mike Chilton on the drive back to Florida.

He reached for the doorknob to Mike's master bedroom again.

The phone trilled again.

It wasn't Detective Collins this time. It was Clifford Terrence Drake Junior.

Wahlman clicked on. "I was going to call you later," he

said. "I haven't had a chance to do the research I need to do yet."

"There's been a change of plans," Drake said. "I'm going to give you an address in Jacksonville. I want you to go there and meet with one of my associates."

"I'm not going anywhere until—"

"I'm going to switch over to a conference call. Don't hang up, okay?"

There was a series of clicks and a short period of static, and then a very familiar voice came on the line, a voice that was somehow hoarse and weary and frantic at the same time.

It was the voice of Mike Chilton.

"Rock, you need to run. Just run, man. Don't worry about me. You need to get out of the country. Today. Get the cash out of my safety deposit box and—"

Click.

Silence.

And then Drake came back on.

He told Wahlman to be at the address in Jacksonville in exactly one hour.

Or else.

18

Wahlman crossed the Buckman Bridge and exited on San Jose Boulevard. He had the .38 with him and the 9mm, minus the silencer, which he'd removed to make the gun easier to carry. Clifford Terrence Drake Junior had arranged for Mike Chilton to be kidnapped, which meant that Clifford Terrence Drake Junior was going to die. Maybe not today, or tomorrow, but soon. That was for sure. As soon as Wahlman could get back to New Orleans, Drake was a dead man. In the meantime, anyone who worked for him was going to get a good old-fashioned Master-at-Arms ass kicking.

At the very least.

Wahlman sped through four yellow lights and one red one, took a right and covered several more blocks in a matter of seconds, driving the pickup like some kind of racecar, downshifting into the curves and flooring it on the straightaways, finally veering into an industrial loop and steering into the abandoned factory where the meeting was supposed to take place.

He got there with about ten minutes to spare.

He climbed out of the truck, stuffed both guns into the back of his waistband, covered the grips with the tails of his shirt. He was supposed to walk to the gate and press the big red button and wait for an escort. But that was not what he did. There were no rules in a situation like this, as far as Wahlman was concerned. His best friend had been abducted, and was being held against his will. All bets were off. No holds barred. So instead of pressing the button and waiting for someone to come, he climbed the fence and walked up a set of concrete steps to the loading dock and entered the factory through one of the big rollup doors, which had been left wide open.

There was a guard standing about five feet inside the door. Average height, average weight, gray coveralls, black ball cap.

Twelve-gauge pump.

"You here to see Mr. Nefangar?" the man asked.

"Maybe," Wahlman said.

"You were supposed to wait outside the gate."

"Yet here I am."

"I'm authorized to shoot you if you give me any trouble."

"You're not going to shoot me. If you were going to shoot me, I'd be dead already. Take me to Nefangar."

"I was supposed to call him when you sounded the buzzer."

"So call him."

"You didn't do what you were supposed to do."

"Want me to climb back over the fence and start over?" Wahlman asked.

"You're a smartass, you know that?"

"Better than being a dumbass, like you."

The guard chuckled. "Just wait," he said. "In less than an hour, you're going to be begging me to shoot you. That's how much pain you're going to be in."

He leaned the shotgun against the wall, pulled a cell phone out of his pocket and punched in a number. While he was waiting for an answer, Wahlman reached around and pulled the .38 out of his waistband, aimed and fired and blew the guard's right kneecap off. The cell phone skittered across the concrete floor as the guy collapsed in a screaming heap.

Wahlman walked over and grabbed the shotgun, and then he picked up the phone and pressed it against his ear.

"Anyone there?" he asked.

"Who is this? McNeal? Was that a gunshot I just heard? Where are you? Where's Wahlman?"

"Who's McNeal?" Wahlman asked. "The guy in the gray coveralls? I'm afraid he's not feeling very well right now. Can I take a message?"

"Wahlman?"

"Nefanger?"

"You just signed your friend's execution order. I hope you know that."

"Let him go," Wahlman said. "Drake doesn't care anything about him. Drake wants me. For whatever reason. I really don't even care anymore. If he's determined to kill me, then he's going to kill me. That's the way it works in the real world. But I'm not going to turn myself over until I know that Mike is safe."

"You're in no position to be making demands," Nefangar said. "I'll kill your friend, and then I'll kill you."

"No you won't. Because like I told McKneeless over there, if you'd wanted to kill me, then I never would have made it through the door. You want to keep me alive for some reason. For a while, anyway. It doesn't really matter why, but I can promise you one thing: I'm going to keep doing a whole lot of damage until you let Mike Chilton go."

Nefangar laughed. "What kind of damage?" he asked.

Wahlman walked over to McNeal, who now seemed to be in shock. Maybe from the blood loss, maybe from the excruciating pain. Maybe from both. Wahlman pressed the barrel of the shotgun against his chest.

Wahlman had never shot a man at point blank range before.

And he'd never shot an incapacitated man at any range.

But then there was a first time for everything.

"This kind of damage," he said, and pulled the trigger.

19

Partially deafened from the blast, Wahlman stood there and fiddled with the phone until he figured out how to turn up the volume.

"What did you do?" Nefangar asked.

"I killed your sentry. Go ahead and send more. I'll kill them too."

"Are you out of your mind?"

"Plenty of places to hide in this building. I'll pick your guys off one at a time until there's nobody left. Then I'll come after you."

Silence for about ten seconds.

"I'm going to call Mr. Drake and ask him how he wants to proceed," Nefangar said. "I'll call you back."

"Try to make it quick," Wahlman said. "I'm starting to get impatient."

Nefangar disconnected.

There were two stainless steel tanks at one end of the room, massive cylindrical things about twenty feet tall and as big around as bedrooms. Above the tanks, and leading down into them, were a pair of motorized mixing blades, huge steel shafts mounted on tresses that had been bolted to the ceiling. There was a stretch of scaffolding along the rear edge of the tanks, with a portable set of stairs pushed up against each side. Above the scaffolding Wahlman could see electrical conduit and copper plumbing, everything caked with grime and exposed in a tangle, like some kind of filthy industrial spaghetti, as if the infrastructural components of the operation had been installed as an afterthought, as if the pipes and valves and wires and junctions had been utilized for a short period of time and then abandoned and left to decay.

Wahlman started walking toward the tanks. He figured if you got both of those things humming real good you could crank out about a hundred and sixty thousand margaritas in no time. Assuming the tanks were five thousand gallons each, and assuming you used eight ounce glasses for the drinks.

Wahlman was good at calculating things like that in his head. In school he'd sometimes been suspected of cheating on math tests, because he always finished quickly and rarely needed to work anything out on paper. He would look at the problems and write down the answers, and then he would spend the rest of the period doodling or daydreaming. It drove his teachers crazy.

He stayed close to the wall as he approached the tanks, trying to keep a low profile in case any more guys in gray coveralls were lurking about. He made it to the mobile steel staircase on the right, tested his weight on the first couple of risers and then climbed up to the catwalk and peered down into one of the tanks through an access hatch. The shiny steel floor was dry, but the air smelled faintly of vinegar. Maybe this had been a salad dressing factory, he thought. He envisioned automatic chutes and conveyor belts and plastic bottles and hoses and nozzles and cardboard boxes stacked on wooden pallets.

And then he wondered why the factory wasn't here anymore. People still ate plenty of salad dressing, so it had to be coming from somewhere. But then maybe something else had been produced here, something that had become obsolete. He was staring down into the tank and thinking about that when the phone trilled again.

"What did he say?" Wahlman asked, assuming it was Nefangar.

"By *he*, I suppose you mean *me*," an unexpected male voice said.

It was Drake.

"I suppose I did," Wahlman said. "I'll tell you the same thing I told Nefangar. I'm not turning myself over until I'm a hundred percent certain that Mike Chilton has been set free."

"I'm on a jet to Florida right now," Drake said. "My clients have insisted that I tend to this matter myself."

"Who are your clients?"

"You wouldn't believe me if I told you."

"Try me."

"Let's just say they're quite perturbed that this situation wasn't taken care of Sunday at the sandwich shop. But it's going to be taken care of today. Definitely."

"Who are your clients?" Wahlman asked again. "I think I have a right to know who's trying to kill me."

"We'll discuss that when I get there. Then again, maybe not. Seems kind of pointless, if you want to know the truth."

Wahlman did want to know the truth, but it seemed increasingly unlikely that Clifford Terrence Drake Junior would ever deliver it in any sort of meaningful way.

"Where's Mike?" Wahlman asked. "I want to see him. Or at least talk to him."

"Your friend is being driven to a different location as we speak. He was Special Forces in the navy, right?"

"Yes. He was a SEAL."

"Then he shouldn't have any problem finding his way out of the Okefenokee Swamp. It might take him a day or two, but he will survive."

"That's your idea of setting him free?"

"I'm afraid that's the best I can do. I can't just take him back to his house, now can I? He might come back to the factory and attempt some kind of daring rescue."

Drake seemed to be enjoying himself. He was having a little fun at Wahlman's expense. His vocal inflection on *daring rescue* made it sound like a melodramatic and silly thing to try.

"How will I know that you really let him go?" Wahlman asked, keeping his own tone serious, refusing to take the bait.

"We'll transmit satellite images to your phone. You'll be able to see the beads of sweat on your friend's face as he tries to make his way out of the swamp."

Live images from cameras in outer space. Close-ups. High-resolution. Ordinary citizens didn't have access to that kind of technology. Which told Wahlman that Drake's clients were not ordinary citizens.

"You're not a lawyer," Wahlman said. "You're some kind of mercenary."

"Who says I can't be both? Now listen very carefully. I'm going to give you some information you'll need to gain access to the satellite feed."

Drake spelled out a user name and a password.

"Who hired you?" Wahlman asked again.

"This thing is bigger than you, or me, or Darrell Renfro, or Allison Bentley. This thing is bigger than big. You need to wrap your head around that, Mr. Wahlman. And you need to wrap your head around the fact that you're going to die today."

Wahlman wanted to wrap Drake's head around something. Maybe one of the steel mixing blades he was staring down at.

"When will I be able to see the pictures of Mike out in the Okefenokee?" he asked.

"Check your phone in about an hour."

"Then what?"

"Then I'll call you and instruct you on exactly what to do next. In the meantime, you should stay where you are, there on the catwalk behind the mixing tanks."

"How did you know—"

"See you soon," Drake said, and disconnected.

20

Drake hadn't given Wahlman much information, but he'd given him some. And along with the other things Wahlman had learned over the past two and a half days, it was enough to piece some things together and formulate a loose hypothesis.

A United States government agency, or a branch of the military, or a foreign government agency or military, had hired a team of mercenaries to kill Renfro and Wahlman, who somehow shared similar fingerprints and the exact same DNA as a former army officer named Jack Reacher. That was it in a nutshell. Which meant that the United States government, or a branch of the military, or a foreign government or military, had something to hide regarding Reacher and Renfro and Wahlman, something that possibly involved some sort of genetic research.

Because according to the results, you and Darrell Renfro and Jack Reacher are all the same person.

Human cloning.

As insane as it sounded, Wahlman couldn't think of anything else it could be.

Detective Collins had said that the lab results were an obvious mistake, but Wahlman didn't think so.

The technology had been around for a long time, and it had been illegal for a long time. Most mainstream scientists considered it unethical, for a variety of reasons. But the fact that it was illegal and unethical didn't mean that it wasn't happening, and it didn't mean that it hadn't been happening back around the time Wahlman was born. There were conspiracy theories to such effect. The tabloids were full of them. Wahlman had never put much stock in those kinds of things, but he supposed it was within the realm of possibility that some of the theories were true.

Clifford Terrence Drake Junior—maybe his real name, maybe not—was the leader of the team of mercenaries. The team had been hired to kill Wahlman and Renfro, and maybe dozens of other clones. Hundreds? Thousands? It sounded improbable and outrageous, but then this whole thing sounded improbable and outrageous. Human duplicates? Why would a government have done such a thing? And why would they have chosen this Jack Reacher fellow as a donor? Was it a random choice, or was there some sort of reasoning behind it?

Those were some of the questions rattling around in Wahlman's brain, although he was doubtful that he would live long enough to find the answers.

But maybe he would. The team of mercenaries had probably only originally consisted of five guys: Drake and Nefangar, the first and second in command; the guy behind Allison's drapes and McNeal, the first and second to die; and one other guy, who was currently transporting Mike Chilton to the Okefenokee Swamp.

Five to start with.

Three remaining.

That was Wahlman's guess, based on his experience with similar groups on similar missions. If you were putting a crew like that together, you didn't want too many people on the payroll, and you didn't want too many people who could testify against you if things went bad. The fewer the better. Drake and Nefangar probably could have handled the job themselves, but they'd chosen to hire the other guys, for whatever reasons.

Five to start with.

Three remaining.

Wahlman's estimate was also based on the fact that nobody else had come after him yet. If there had been more hired guns hanging out somewhere in the factory, they would have come and tried to kill him by now. Two, three, a dozen, it didn't matter. If they had been here, they would have come.

Which meant that Nefangar was probably alone right now.

Wahlman thought about going after him, decided not to. Mostly out of concern for Mike. Also, it was indeed a big building, and there were indeed plenty of places to hide. And Nefangar was probably monitoring Wahlman's movements. Wahlman hadn't been able to spot any security cameras yet, but he knew they were there. It was the only way Drake could have known that he was on the catwalk behind the tanks.

Which was the safest place for him to be right now.

Wahlman hadn't climbed up there out of curiosity. He'd chosen the position as a tactical defense strategy. If his estimate regarding the number of mercenaries was wrong, or if Drake and Nefangar somehow managed to call in some reinforcements, at least he would have a fighting chance from the elevated position. Maybe more than a fighting chance, considering the assortment of weapons he'd accumulated over the past twenty-four hours. The .38 and the 9mm and the shotgun. He wasn't equipped to fend off an army, but he wasn't exactly helpless either.

The phone made a little tinkling sound that Wahlman hadn't heard before. He looked at the display and saw that Drake had sent him a text message. No correspondence, just a link to a website. When Wahlman tapped on the link, a login window popped up. He entered the user name and password Drake had given him earlier, and the next thing he saw was a wide grassy area flanked on each side by small ponds and massive oak trees. He zoomed in. A little black dot appeared to be moving slowly across the grassy area. He zoomed in some more, closer and closer, zeroing in on the little black dot, which turned out to be a man, but not the man Wahlman had been expecting to see. Not Mike Chilton, his best friend in the world, but someone else, someone he'd never seen before. The man was running, sweating, grunting, seemingly on the verge of collapse, pushing himself forward as if someone was chasing him, someone who meant to do him great harm. Then, suddenly, something swooped in behind him, a flying object, a helicopter, a very small one, the rotors churning in an arc no bigger than a pizza pan. The man started zigzagging toward the tree line in one last frantic effort to survive, but it was no use. The copter dove down a little closer to the ground and leveled out directly behind the man and there was a short burst of gunfire and that was it.

The display went dark for a few seconds, and then another scene appeared. Another man running, sweating, grunting. This time it was Mike Chilton. Wahlman recognized him, even though his head had been shaved completely bald. Mike was wearing the shirt Wahlman had given him for his birthday a couple of years ago. It was torn and dirty and soaked with sweat. The miniature helicopter was no longer visible, but Wahlman could hear the motor whirring somewhere in the distance, perhaps just out of camera range.

The phone made the little tinkling sound again.

It was another text message from Drake:

Just wanted to show off our handy-dandy little drone. Just so there's no misunderstanding, just in case you were thinking you might be able to escape now that Mike Chilton has been set free. From this point forward, if you do anything other than what we tell you to do—and I mean exactly what we tell you to do—your friend will die.

The phone trilled. It was Nefangar.

"Did you get the message from Mr. Drake?" he asked.

"I got it," Wahlman said.

"Good. I want you to climb down the set of stairs to your right. You'll see a door that says AUTHORIZED PERSONNEL

ONLY. Open the door and walk all the way to the end of the hallway and take a left."

"Then what?"

"Don't worry about *then what*. Just do as you're told. And leave your weapons there on the catwalk. The twelve-gauge and both of the handguns. Any sort of failure to cooperate will result in the immediate execution of your friend."

"We're kind of back to square one, aren't we?" Wahlman said. "Even if I do cooperate, how do I know you're not going to—"

Nefangar hung up.

Wahlman thought about staying on the catwalk and trying to fight it out. But if he did, Mike would die for sure. Going along with Drake and Nefangar wouldn't guarantee a better outcome, but it would give Mike some time to think. He was a SEAL. He was an expert at surviving, even when the odds seemed insurmountable. And maybe Drake and Nefangar would keep their word and let him live. Or at least not gun him down with the drone. At least give him a chance to navigate his way out of the swamp.

With that in mind, Wahlman set all three of his guns down on the steel platform and headed toward the stairs.

21

When Wahlman got to the end of the hallway and took a left, a man was standing there waiting for him.

A small man with a large gun.

A .44 magnum.

Nickel plated with black grips. Barrel as fat as a soup can.

"Nefangar?" Wahlman said.

"Don't talk. Drop the phone. I want you face down on the floor with your hands laced behind your head. Do it. Now."

"You sounded bigger when I talked to you earlier. Is Drake a pipsqueak too?"

Nefangar reached into his pocket and pulled out a cell phone.

"I have a text ready to be sent out," he said. "All I have to do is tap the *SEND* button, and your friend is dead."

Wahlman weighed his options. He could go for the gun and hope Nefangar didn't have the presence of mind to send the text, or he could go for the phone and hope Nefangar didn't have the presence of mind to blow his brains out.

Then he remembered something Mike Chilton had told him one time: *when an opponent has the upper hand, sometimes you just have to play it cool for a while. Sometimes you just have to wait for the right opportunity to present itself. As long as you're still breathing, there's a chance the tables will turn. When they do, don't hesitate. Strike fast. Strike hard. Get out.*

It wasn't anything you were going to find in any sort of field manual. It was something Mike had learned from experience. From being in situations that seemed hopeless.

In his formal training, Wahlman had been taught to avoid capture at all costs.

But this time the cost was just too high.

Wahlman dropped Allison's cell phone, heard the display window crack when the device hit the concrete. He got down on the floor and laced his hands behind his head, immediately felt Nefangar's knee come down hard on the lower part of his back. Nefangar dug his bony little thumbs into some pressure points on Wahlman's hands and forced them down to the center of his ribcage and secured them at the wrists with nylon zip ties.

"Seems like you might have done this kind of thing before," Wahlman said.

"Get up."

Wahlman rolled over and rose to a standing position, again noticing what a small man Nefangar was. Five-five, maybe five-six. Skinny and pale. He wore an outfit identical to McNeal's. Gray coveralls and a black hat.

"You look like you could use some vitamins," Wahlman said. "Or a blood transfusion or something."

Nefangar pointed the .44 at Wahlman's chest. "Turn around and start walking," he said. "Slowly. All the way to the door at the end of the hallway."

"You're pretty tough with a gun in your hand. Put it down and see if I don't kick your ass all the way to the door at the end of the hallway."

"Move!"

Wahlman turned around and started walking. When he got to the end of the hallway, Nefangar instructed him to step to the right and place the toes of his boots against the baseboard and his forehead against the wall.

"So you can shoot me in the back of the head?" Wahlman asked. "So you don't have to look into my eyes when you do it?"

"You're starting to get on my nerves."

"That's okay. You're starting to get on mine too."

"Mr. Drake will be here shortly. Then you will die. Slowly and painfully, if I have anything to say about it. In the meantime, I need you stand against the wall while I open this door. Then I'm going to follow you into the room on the other side of it. That's one way we can do it. The other way is for me to shatter the bones in your feet with a couple of .44 slugs and drag you into the room."

"I guess I'll go for Option One," Wahlman said.

"Good choice."

Wahlman turned and edged his toes up against the baseboard, and then he leaned in and pressed his forehead against the painted sheetrock. Nefangar's keys jingled as he pulled them out of his pocket, and they jingled some more as he turned them over in his hand and searched for the one that would open the door.

Which presented a potential opportunity.

One of Nefangar's hands was busy fumbling with the keys, and the other was busy holding the unwieldy handgun, which meant that the cell phone with the fatal *SEND* button was out of the picture for the moment. Probably in a pocket. Within reach, but it would take some time to fish it out. At least a couple of seconds.

As long as you're still breathing, there's a chance the tables will turn. When they do, don't hesitate. Strike fast. Strike hard. Get out.

Wahlman waited until he heard the key slide into the slot and the deadbolt click open, and then he pivoted ninety degrees and lowered his left shoulder and rammed into Nefangar's right arm, hammering him with tremendous force, tenderizing him like a piece of raw meat. The keys tinkled brassily to the concrete floor, Nefangar's left ribcage slammed crunchily against the steel doorframe, and the .44 magnum discharged harmlessly into the section of sheetrock Wahlman had been leaning against.

Wahlman got down on the floor and arched his back and bent his knees and wriggled his restrained hands to the front where he could use them. He grabbed the keys and stuffed them into his pocket, and then he stood and pressed his boot against Nefangar's wrist and bent over and pried the revolver out of his fingers. Nefangar tried to resist, but it seemed that the little bit of strength he had left was being used to draw air into his right lung—the only one that was still functioning at full capacity.

Wahlman reached into Nefangar's left front pants pocket and carefully pulled out the cell phone.

"You're going to die," Nefangar grunted.

"We're all going to die," Wahlman said. "Some of us sooner than others. You sooner than most."

He pressed the barrel of the .44 against Nefangar's forehead.

Cocked the hammer back.

"Wait," Nefangar said. "I can arrange it so you'll know for sure that Mike Chilton is safe."

"How can you do that?"

"I'll show you how to disable the drone. Then you can pinpoint Mike's exact location and send some cops or whoever out there to help him."

"Okay. Show me."

"First you have to promise that you're not going to shoot me."

"Who was the guy running from the drone earlier?" Wahlman asked. "The one who got shot in the back."

"That was our man," Nefangar said. "He drove Chilton out to the swamp."

"Why did you kill him?"

"He made a stupid mistake. He was a liability."

"Show me how to disable the drone."

"First you have to promise that you're not going to—"

"Okay. I promise."

Wahlman gently released the hammer and slid the humongous revolver into his waistband. Nobody needed a gun that big, he thought. It was like carrying an anvil.

"Use my cell phone to access the satellite site," Nefangar said. "But don't log in. I'm going to give you a special user name and password."

"I'm going to need my hands," Wahlman said. "Do you have something I can cut these ties off with?"

Nefangar nodded. He slowly and painstakingly slid two fingers into his pocket and pulled out a small lock-blade knife. He tried to open it, didn't have the strength. He finally gave up and tossed the knife on the floor near Wahlman's feet.

Wahlman bent over and picked it up.

Opened it.

Examined it.

Noticed that there were some tiny blackish-red flakes where the blade locked into the handle.

Blood, he thought. Most likely from Darrell Renfro's abdomen.

He sawed the zip ties off and folded the blade back into the handle and slid the knife into his pocket. Then he pulled out Nefangar's phone.

"The first thing you need to do is retract the kill command," Nefangar said.

"How to I do that?"

"See the button that says *SEND*?"

"Yes."

"If you tap it two times in quick succession, your friend will die in a matter of seconds."

"I obviously don't want that to happen."

"Right. So what you need to do is tap the button *three*

times in quick succession. That will cause the drone to return to its base to wait for further commands."

"I thought you said I could disable the drone completely," Wahlman said.

"You have to send it back to its base first."

"How do I know you're telling the truth? I do I know that tapping the button three times won't dial in the kill command?"

"I'm trying to save my own skin," Nefangar said. "That's what this is all about, remember? Why would I lie?"

Wahlman nodded.

He looked down at the display screen.

Stared at the *SEND* button.

Thought about it.

Thought about it some more.

And then he tapped the button three times.

22

Nothing happened.

"How do I know Mike's okay?" Wahlman asked. "How do I know the drone went back to its base?"

"Go to the website," Nefangar said. "There's a link in my bookmarks."

Wahlman found the link and accessed the website for the satellite feed.

"I'm looking at the login window," he said. "I need the special user name and password you told me about."

Nefangar started laughing. "There's no special user name and password," he said. "I made that up. Why should I help you get what you want? I was dead the second you took my gun. Look at me. I need a doctor. I'm going to need to be hospitalized. Drake's not going to let me live. I'm of no use to him now."

"What are you saying?"

"I'm saying that your friend Mike Chilton is dead. And I'm saying that you're the one who killed him. If you had cooperated, everything would have been all right. We would have let Chilton go. But you had to be the big hero, didn't you? My life is over now, Mr. Wahlman, but so is yours. There's no escape. Even if you manage to get away from Drake, there's still no escape. Our clients aren't the kind of people who give up. Ever. They'll hire someone else to track you down, or maybe they'll do it themselves this time. They'll find you. Tomorrow, next week, whenever."

Wahlman reared back and threw Nefangar's cell phone toward the end of the hallway. He threw it hard, overhand, like a baseball, and then he pulled the .44 from his waistband, cocked the hammer back, aimed the barrel at Nefangar's face.

"Who are your clients?" he asked.

"Seems like you have some anger management issues. You might want to see someone about that."

"Who are your clients?"

"I'm sure you have a lot of questions," Nefangar said. "Like how it went down with Renfro. Like how we placed one of our guys in Allison Bentley's hotel room. Like how we drained your bank account, or why any of this is even happening. With Renfro, it was supposed to look like an accident. McNeal and I followed—"

Wahlman jammed the barrel of the revolver into Nefangar's mouth, breaking several of his front teeth in the process.

"I don't care about any of that shit," Wahlman said. "Not anymore. You think I'm going to stand here and listen to you talk until Drake gets here? I'm going to ask you one more time. Who are your clients?"

Nefangar started gagging. Wahlman pulled the gun out of his mouth. Nefangar turned his head to the side and coughed out some blood and tooth fragments.

"You want to know who hired us?" he said, his speech wet and garbled and nearly incomprehensible. "Why? So you can go after them? It's not going to work. They're too big. The issue they're trying to keep secret is too big. You don't have a chance."

"As long as I'm still breathing, I still have a chance," Wahlman said.

And then he took two steps backward and emptied the revolver into Nefangar's chest.

Which he knew right away was a big mistake. He had allowed his emotions to get the best of him. He should have kept at least one bullet for contingencies.

Because when he turned to run back out to the tanks, to retrieve the weapons he'd left on the catwalk, he saw a man with an Uzi standing at the end of the hallway.

"Allow me to introduce myself," the man said. "Clifford Terrence Drake Junior, Attorney at Law."

Wahlman didn't know what was behind the door Nefangar had opened a few minutes ago, but he knew it couldn't possibly be any worse than what he was facing now. He dropped the .44 and dove toward the door and rolled into the room on the other side of it, barely beating a short burst of rounds from Drake's machinegun. The bullets pinged off the concrete and thudded into the wood and drywall as Wahlman scurried back to the threshold and slammed the door shut and secured the deadbolt.

There was another door on the other side of the room. Two entrances from two different hallways. Typical for this kind of setup, Wahlman thought. A common area for staff meetings and educational presentations and whatnot. He'd seen plenty of similar arrangements on naval bases, and even on ships.

Drake was still on the other side of the door that Nefangar had opened with the key. Wahlman could hear him over there ramming it with his shoulder, trying to bust through the frame. Maybe he had never been to the factory before. Maybe he didn't know about the double entrance. Wahlman hoped he didn't, because the second door represented his only chance of getting out of there alive. He stayed low, belly-crawling past a conference table and a file cabinet and a small steel safe, almost making it to the door before looking back and noticing that he was leaving a trail of blood.

He'd been hit.

Left hamstring, several inches above the knee joint.

The extreme adrenaline rush from the fight-or-flight response must have kept him from feeling the bullet as it went in, but he could certainly feel it now. Like someone holding a soldering iron to the back of his leg. He reached up and unlocked the deadbolt, opened the door and crawled out into the hallway.

Drake was still trying to break through the door on the other side. Wahlman could hear him. Banging with his shoulder, kicking with his foot. Probably thinking that he had plenty of time. Probably thinking that he had Wahlman trapped.

Drake could have tried blasting the lock off with the Uzi, but Wahlman supposed he was too smart for that. It was highly unlikely for a bullet to strike a lock mechanism in the precise manner it would need to in order to break it open. What was more likely was that one or more of the rounds shot at the lock would ricochet back and hit the shooter. Not to mention the ammunition that would be wasted. Trying to blast a lock with a gun was an all-around fail most of the time, a notion that was dispelled during the first week of any sort of serious firearms training.

Wahlman stood and started limping toward the end of the hallway, toward the turn that would lead him back to the production area, warm blood from the gunshot wound trickling down the back of his leg in a steady stream. The injury was serious, but it could have been a lot worse. If the bullet had clipped his femoral artery, he probably would have bled out by now. The hole in his leg hurt like crazy, but it didn't present an immediate threat to his life.

He made it to the end of the hallway, took a right down a shorter corridor, pushed his way through the heavy steel door, out into the big room where the big tanks were. Now it was just a matter of getting over to the stairs and climbing up to the catwalk and retrieving the weapons he'd left there. Easier said than done when it felt like a handful of razorblades were being jammed into the back of his leg. He hobbled along the edge of the factory floor as fast as he could, losing a few more drops of blood with every excruciating step.

By the time he got to the portable steel staircase on the

right side of the tanks, the one he'd used previously, the pain in his leg had subsided some, which was good, but then he saw that the staircase had been pulled away from the catwalk, which was not good. Now there was a gap between the top step and the horizontal platform. Ten feet or so. Too far to jump, especially with a shredded hamstring. Wahlman backed up far enough to see that the staircase on the left had been moved as well. He figured Drake must have pulled the units away from the platform on his way in. Motivation unknown. Maybe he'd thought that Wahlman was still up there. Or maybe he'd planned ahead, envisioning the possibility of the scenario that was playing out now. Smart. And if that was the case, it probably wouldn't be long until he came out to the production area to take a look, regardless of whether or not he managed to break through the door to the conference room.

Which meant that Wahlman needed to hurry.

He tried wheeling the staircase back into position, quickly realized that there was a braking mechanism on it somewhere that needed to be released. He found the lever and yanked it back and scooted the stairs closer to the catwalk. Not quite flush, but close enough. He mounted the first step and immediately fell back and landed on his ass.

The pain in his leg had subsided because his leg had gone numb.

No longer able to stand on two feet, Wahlman started crawling up the steps, gripping the back of each riser with his fingers and pushing himself upward with his right leg. His heart was racing and he felt weaker than he'd ever felt in his life. He was dizzy and he couldn't remember what day it was and he knew that he was going to die if he didn't get medical attention soon. Just a few more feet, he thought. Just a few more feet to the top of the stairs. Then he could defend himself. It was just Drake now. Just one guy. No problem. All he needed to do was make it up to the catwalk.

And then, suddenly, he was there.

And just as suddenly, a familiar voice echoed from the other side of the production area.

"Now I've got you," Drake said.

23

A deafening barrage of automatic rifle fire blasted through the cavernous space, a staccato series of earsplitting explosions, like a brick of firecrackers linked with a single fuse. Wahlman scrabbled toward the section of the catwalk where he'd left the guns. The .38 and the 9mm and the twelve gauge pump.

But they weren't there.

They were gone.

Drake must have done something with them before he moved the staircases.

Wahlman pulled himself up to the lip of the tank and peered down into the same access hatch he'd peered down into earlier, thinking the enormous container would have been a convenient place for Drake to ditch the weapons.

Same faint smell of vinegar, same shiny steel floor.

No guns.

They weren't at the bottom of the tank, because they were on top of the tank. Near the edge, in front, about twelve feet from where Wahlman was standing. Drake had probably tossed them out there, thinking he would come back for them later. Which made sense. The fewer pieces of evidence left behind, the better. And it would be much quicker and easier to retrieve these particularly incriminating items from the top of the tank than it would from the bottom.

Thinking ahead again.

Smart.

But not really. Arrogant was more like it. Drake had never anticipated Wahlman escaping and getting enough of a head start to be in the position he was in right now.

He'd underestimated his opponent.

A big mistake, and now he was going to pay for it.

Wahlman had been on the verge of passing out, but a fresh surge of adrenaline had brought him back to a high state of alertness. He felt reenergized, but he knew it wouldn't last. He'd lost a lot of blood, and the only way to fix that was to replace it. He needed someone to dig the bullet out and stitch the wound and transfuse him with two or three units of packed red blood cells.

But first things first.

The top of the tank was filthy, coated with the same greasy dust as the plumbing and electrical conduit. Wahlman climbed up there and started crawling toward the edge, his numb left leg and the slimy black film on the tank making it ten times more difficult than it should have been.

Somewhere around the halfway point, Drake opened up with the Uzi again. Bullets drum-rolled off the upper part of the tank, leaving trails of bright orange sparks as they tore through the ceiling.

140

Wahlman was hesitant to proceed toward the edge of the tank now. Toward the weapons that represented a potential way out of this, but also toward the hailstorm of machinegun rounds that represented potential instant death. He was hesitant to proceed, but he knew it was the only possible way he was going to survive. If he stayed where he was, he would die. He would eventually lose consciousness from the blood loss, or Drake would eventually climb up to the catwalk and finish him off with the Uzi. One of those two things would happen if he stayed where he was. It was only a matter of which would happen first. So he had to continue moving forward, even though it went against his instincts. He figured his odds of making it out of the factory alive were about a million to one at this point, but a million to one was better than a million to zero.

He kept inching toward the edge.

Grunting.

Sweating.

Wheezing.

And then the fingers on his right hand closed around the grips of the 9mm semiautomatic pistol. Finally. Now he could defend himself. He waited for another short burst from Drake's Uzi, aimed toward the muzzle flash and pulled the trigger.

And nothing happened.

He turned the gun over and stared into the hollow space where the magazine was supposed to be. No magazine, no bullet in the chamber. He tossed the pistol aside and grabbed the shotgun, checked it over and saw right away that the ammunition had been ejected from it as well.

Which left the revolver.

The .38 he'd bought in the freezer at Dena Jo's.

He grabbed the gun and aimed it down toward the area Drake had been shooting from and squeezed the trigger.

Nothing.

The .38 was empty too.

Drake had removed the ammunition from all three guns.

Thinking ahead.

Smart.

He hadn't underestimated his opponent after all. He'd done everything just right.

And now the only thing Wahlman could do was lie there and wait.

But maybe not.

He still had the folding lock-blade knife he'd taken from Nefangar.

It wasn't much, but it was better than nothing.

He reached into his pocket to get it as Drake's footsteps creaked rhythmically up the staircase.

24

Drake was moving slowly, cautiously. It took him a minute or so to make it to the section of the catwalk behind the tank on the right. Now he was standing directly across from Wahlman, who was still lying on top of the tank, near the edge.

Drake slammed a fresh magazine into the Uzi, and then he aimed the barrel at Wahlman's core.

"You win," Wahlman said. "You killed Darrel Renfro, and Allison Bentley, and your own man out in the swamp, and Mike Chilton. Now you're going to kill me, and there's nothing I can do to stop you. All I want to know is why."

"There's no short answer for that," Drake said.

Wahlman kept his eyes glued to Drake's right index finger. The one on the trigger.

"Then give me the long answer," he said.

"What's the point?"

"At least tell me who hired you. At least give me that."

Drake looked at his watch.

"My plane back to New Orleans isn't scheduled to take

off for another couple of hours," he said. "I suppose I could stand here and chat for a while. Watch you slowly bleed to death. Or I could finish you off right now. I'll get paid the same regardless, so it really doesn't matter to me. What do you want to know?"

"Everything."

Drake laughed. "If I were in your position, I suppose I would want to know everything too. Delay the inevitable for as long as possible. Maybe the cavalry will show up just in the nick of time. Maybe I'll drop dead of a heart attack. Anything could happen, right? But we both know that nothing like that is going to happen. And we both know that the little knife in your left hand isn't going to do you any good, and that the thirty-eight revolver in your right hand isn't going to do you any good. Or maybe you haven't tried the gun yet. Maybe you don't know. Go ahead. Aim it at me and pull the trigger. There aren't any bullets in it. I threw them away. All six of them. I discarded the ammunition from the other guns up there beside you as well. So all you really have is the little knife. Which isn't going to help you, no matter how long I stand here and talk. What are you planning to do? Throw it at me? Hope it sticks in my throat or something? Get real."

"Like I said, you win. I'm not delusional, Drake. I just want to know why all this had to happen."

Drake nodded. "Fair enough," he said. "Okay. Everything. Well, believe it or not, it all started in nineteen eighty-three, at Ramstein Air Force Base in Germany. Quite a few American soldiers and officers were there being treated for injuries sustained during an attack in Beirut, Lebanon. During one of the routine a.m. blood draws, an army general called in an order for forty extra vials to be taken from forty of the American patients. Nobody's sure exactly why he called in the order, but he did. The vials were labeled and shipped to the States, where the cells were analyzed and then cryogenically preserved in a secret underground laboratory in Colorado. Fast forward seventy-four years. Two thousand fifty-seven. A lot of things had changed by then. Politically. Financially. Technologically. An independent group of scientists petitioned the United States Army for funds and a venue to conduct a series of experiments on human cloning. It was illegal, of course, just as it is now, but the army said they would go along with it—in an unofficial capacity—as long as no living person was used as a donor. One of the scientists did a little research and discovered that the preserved samples from nineteen eighty-three were still in the deepfreeze, right there in the lab they wanted to use. Long story short, a total of eighty fetuses were produced, two from each specimen. Out of those eighty, only two survived. Both from an officer named Jack Reacher."

"So I was one of the two," Wahlman said. "And Renfro was the other."

"Correct. Two surrogate mothers were hired, strict non-disclosure agreements and all that, but at some point during the pregnancies, the army decided to bail on the experiment, leaving the independent group of scientists with no funding and no venue. You and Renfro were given fake identities and fake histories and sent to orphanages in different states. That should have been the end of it. You should have been left to live out your lives. No harm, no foul. Happily ever after. Unfortunately, the army recently discovered that an electronic file containing a thousand or so pages of classified data might have been hacked into. They're not sure, but they think some of the correspondence between the geneticists and the officer in charge of the clandestine funding might have been included in that data. So they're basically trying to cover their tracks, trying to eliminate any sort of evidence that would link them to the illegal study."

"Why don't they just kill the hackers?" Wahlman asked.

"That would be one way to approach the problem. Unfortunately, they have no idea who the hackers are. In fact, they don't really know if there *are* any hackers. It's just a strong suspicion, based on—"

"So they hired you to kill Renfro and me as a precautionary measure? Just in case some of that classified data was breached? That's insane."

"What can I say? It's the army. They pay well, I can tell you that. And now that Nefangar and the other three guys are gone, I'll get to keep it all for myself. One squeeze of the trigger, and I get to retire. In style."

"One squeeze of the trigger," Wahlman said.

And as he was saying it, he discreetly flicked his wrist and whizzed the little lock-blade knife off the side of the tank. It toppled down through the dirty pipes and the electrical conduit, making enough noise to create a momentary diversion. When Drake turned his head slightly to the right, the barrel of the Uzi shifted slightly to the right as well.

Which gave Wahlman just enough time to aim the .38 and blast a hole through the left side of Drake's jaw.

One bullet was all it took. Which was a good thing, because one bullet was all Wahlman had. He'd found it in the bottom of his pocket a few minutes ago, when he'd reached in for the knife, leftover from the extras he'd taken out when he first opened the box of shells in Allison's car.

An extremely expensive box of shells, but worth every penny.

Strike fast.

Strike hard.

And now it was time to get out.

Wahlman crawled back over to the catwalk and used Drake's cell phone to call a friend—a retired navy surgeon who owed him a favor.

25

Four days later, Wahlman was sitting on a bus, traveling on I-75, somewhere between Atlanta, Georgia and Chattanooga, Tennessee, staring out at the rural landscape and wondering what he was going to do, how he was going to live.

Our clients aren't the kind of people who give up. Ever. They'll hire someone else to track you down, or maybe they'll do it themselves this time. They'll find you. Tomorrow, next week, whenever.

Nefangar was right. They weren't going to give up.

The United States Army. Not the entire branch of the service, of course. Probably some sort of special research division. Isolated. Rogue. Working in their own little bubble. Trying to cover their own little asses, conspiring to conceal the division's involvement in an experiment that took place decades ago.

Which didn't really make sense.

Wahlman was doubtful that it was just a matter of eliminating a pair of lookalikes who'd grown up in separate orphanages. Maybe there were more clones running around somewhere. Maybe it was something else. Drake had said that this thing was bigger than all the people involved. Bigger than big, he'd said. And if that was the case, there had to be more to it. Way more. The cover-up had to involve something that was happening right now. Something that would jeopardize the careers of the personnel working on it right now. Wahlman figured that he and Renfro were just the tip of the iceberg. He had no idea how deep it all went, but he intended to find out, and he intended to use the information as a bargaining chip. Maybe threaten to take it all to the media. The people who were trying to kill him obviously wanted to play hardball, but that was okay. He would give them a game. At the very least, he would go down swinging. He figured it was the only potential pathway back to any sort of normalcy.

Not that things would ever return to the way they were before all this happened. He knew now that his entire life had been a lie. No mother, no father, no car accident. He'd been produced in a lab, grown inside a woman who'd rented her body to the army for nine months. A woman who had probably never been allowed to hold him after he was born. His entire life had been a lie, but he could deal with that. In a way, it eliminated some of the bitterness he'd held onto since childhood. Since there never were any actual grandparents or aunts or uncles or cousins, there were no reasons for Wahlman to be angry at them. So the whole bogus personal history thing wasn't bothering him much. It was the loss of Mike Chilton that he was having a problem dealing with. It never should have happened. It was a totally unnecessary tragedy, and it was a weight that Wahlman would carry around for the rest of his life.

He had convalesced at the surgeon's house for two days, and during that time he'd made some phone calls. He'd spoken to Detective Collins, who told him that Walter Babineaux had regained consciousness and had given the department detailed descriptions of the men who shot him, neither of whom looked anything like Wahlman.

"So we've dropped the charges on that one," Collins had said. "But we still need to talk to you regarding the shooting at the hotel."

"I already told you what happened. It was self-defense."

"You left the scene in a hurry. You took the woman's cell phone with you. We can't just let it go. You know that, as well as I do. We need you to come in and make a formal statement. We'll have to book you, but if everything points toward self-defense, then naturally we'll drop those charges as well. And we're still waiting for—"

"I'm going to have to disappear for a while," Wahlman said. "But not because of that. Get with the Jacksonville Sheriff's Office. Three men were found shot to death in an abandoned factory day before yesterday. Bad guys. Assassins. The guy you found in Allison Bentley's hotel room was working with them. I was the target. I'm pretty sure Allison was involved too. I'm pretty sure she sold me out."

"What are you talking about?"

"She owed a guy ten thousand dollars. She was desperate to get her hands on the money. The guys who were trying to kill me might have found out about that, might have offered to clear the debt in exchange for a quick favor. All she had to do was let one of them come into her room and hide behind the drapes for a while. I've thought about it, and I'm pretty sure that was the only way it could have happened. Maybe Allison didn't know the guy was planning to kill me. Maybe they told her he was just going to rough me up or something. I don't know."

"Who did she owe money to?" Collins asked.

"Guy named Tanner. He's a loan shark. He also runs a business called Dena Jo's Old Fashioned Ice Cream. It was where I bought the .38 that I killed the guy in Allison's room with."

"Tanner. I'll check him out."

"Also, I think I have the knife that was used to kill Darrell Renfro. I'm going to overnight it to you in a padded envelope. It belonged to one of the guys at the factory. Guy named Nefangar. I don't know if that's his real name. Get your forensics team to check it out."

Wahlman had disconnected then. He hadn't been able to think of anything else he needed to talk to Collins about. The results of the repeated DNA tests weren't especially important anymore. Not to Wahlman. He knew for sure now that the initial results had been correct, that he was an exact genetic replica of a man named Jack Reacher. *He was an officer in the army. Special Investigations. Served thirteen years. Apparently he was involved in some questionable activities after he got out.* Wahlman had been thinking about that, thinking he might like to learn more about Jack

Reacher someday, maybe take the time to research some of those questionable activities—if anything had ever been written about them.

A rectangular green sign with reflective white letters said *CHATTANOOGA, 46 MILES*. Wahlman was hungry, and his leg was hurting. The surgeon had given him some pain pills, but they didn't help much. Mostly they just made him feel groggy, and he didn't like that. He needed to stay alert while he was traveling. He needed to be aware of his surroundings. His life depended on it.

He had a little over three thousand dollars in his pocket, but he knew it wouldn't last long. Maybe a month. Cheap hotels, diners, fast food joints. Bus tickets, train tickets, maybe thumbing it sometimes. His retirement check had been credited to his checking account on Tuesday, as scheduled, and he'd managed to close the account and withdraw the balance, but there was no way he could continue receiving the direct deposits every month. No way to do any sort of business that would leave a paper trail. No way to have a permanent address or an automobile.

No way to do anything except run.

And keep running.

Maybe forever.

And try to find out what Drake had meant by bigger than big.

Thanks so much for reading DEAD RINGER!

For occasional updates and special offers, please visit my website and sign up for my newsletter.

My Nicholas Colt thriller series includes nine full-length novels: COLT, LADY 52, POCKET-47, CROSSCUT, SNUFF TAG 9, KEY DEATH, BLOOD TATTOO, SYCAMORE BLUFF, and THE JACK REACHER FILES: FUGITIVE (Previously Published as ANNEX 1).

THE JACK REACHER FILES: VELOCITY takes the series in a new direction, and sets the stage for THE BLOOD NOTEBOOKS.

And now, for the first time, 4 NICHOLAS COLT NOVELS have been published together in a box set at a special low price.

All of my books are lendable, so feel free to share them with a friend at no additional cost.

All reviews are much appreciated!

Thanks again, and happy reading!

Jude

9 781541 254343